DYSNOMIA

Max,
I hope you enjoy
reading my book.
Jenny Story

Library and Archives Canada Cataloguing in Publication

Story, Jenny, 1993-, author
    Dysnomia : outcasts on a distant moon / Jenny Story.

Issued in print and electronic formats.
ISBN 978-1-77141-103-5 (pbk.).--ISBN 978-1-77141-104-2
(html)

    I. Title.

PS8637.T6765D97 2015   jC813'.6   C2014-908004-2
                                            C2014-908005-0

Outcasts on a Distant Moon

DYSNOMIA

Jenny Story

First Published in Canada 2015 by Influence Publishing

Book Cover Design: Trista Baldwin
Illustrator: Jenny Story
Cover Night Sky Illustration: Venomxbaby, venomxbaby.deviantart.com
Editor: Mary Rosenblum
Assistant Editor: Susan Kehoe
Production Editor: Jennifer Kaleta
Typeset: Greg Salisbury
Portrait Photographer: Amanda Waschuk

DISCLAIMER: This book is a work of fiction. Names, characters, places or incidents are either the product of the author's imagination or are used fictitiously. Any resemblance to actual persons, living or dead, events, or locales is entirely coincidental. Readers of this publication agree that neither Jenny Story nor her publisher will be held responsible or liable for damages that may be alleged or resulting directly or indirectly from the reading of this publication.

I would like to dedicate this book to my mother,
for always having my back.

Testimonials

"Jenny Story is a powerful new voice in YA fantasy."
Bennett R. Coles, Winner of the 2013 Cygnus Award for Science Fiction

"Jenny has beautifully been able to infuse her own strength, ambition, and heart into this page-turning fantasy tale."
Betty Watson, Author of *What can Jordyn do?* and *On a Day in Brandon MB 9/9/99*

"Jenny has been an inspiration to many young people and is now adding to her already successful life story by writing this imaginative and fascinating tale."
Sarah McLean, VP Productions, Powerhouse Theatrical Society

"Jenny's determination, perseverance, and creativity are an inspiration to all of us."
Barry Ward, President, Bardel Entertainment

Acknowledgements

I would like to thank my parents, my brother Chris, and my best buddy, my dog Sparkles, who have always been there for me. Thank you also to the rest of my family, teachers, and friends who have supported me. I would also like to thank Bernadette Saquibal who told my mom and me about Influence Publishing. A big thank you to Julie Salisbury for accepting my book and Gulnar Patel and the rest of the crew at Influence. Also to Mary Rosenblum, for all her time in working with me on editing my book and Trista Baldwin's hard work on the book cover and author photo.

Contents

Dedication
Testimonials
Acknowledgements

— Chapter One —

The Chase

Sitting, waiting for something to happen. I peered through my purple sunglasses and covered my face with today's newspaper. Waiting for a signal from my partners. But everything was still and normal in the food court. People were eating, talking amongst themselves, and enjoying their day. My mission, along with my partners, was to find and arrest Don Franko. It sounds like a silly name but when it comes to being a thief, he's the best of the best in Jurassic. He has robbed four banks, six jewellery stores, and managed to steal a couple of jewels from our Princess Rose's castle.

I looked over to the boys, Eli and Knuckles, sitting to my right at another table. Then at Sheena, who was fairly close to them, sitting at a booth. But nothing was happening.

Suddenly Eli flicked his newspaper twice. Bingo, he was here.

Don Franko was sitting down, eating a sandwich, and reading the newspaper. He was a very big man with a few wisps of black hair on his head. You could barely see his legs because his tummy covered them. How somebody like him managed to steal from all those places I'll never know.

Everyone looked at me, waiting for my command. I flicked my hair, giving them the signal to charge in and arrest him. Eli, Knuckles, and I closed in while Sheena ran out in front of him.

"Don Franko!" shouted Sheena. "You are under arrest for burglary."

Don Franko grabbed a ketchup bottle and squeezed it. Ketchup squirted all over Sheena's face.

Sheena screamed and he made a run for it.

"Get him!" I shouted. We ran after him. My team ran out the exit door near the food court while I chased after him. He ran past all the clothing stores until he saw a young man with a bookstore on wheels. Don Franko pushed him down.

"Hey!" the young man yelled.

"Sorry kid," said Don Franko with a smirk on his face. "But I've got to run."

He grabbed the cart and shoved it towards me. Running at full speed, I tried to dodge it, but a corner hit me in the back and knocked me to the ground. I fell so hard that I felt a friction burn on my right arm.

"Don Franko is really going to regret messing with me," I growled and ran again. I'm a pretty fast runner so it wasn't hard to spot Don Franko running into the left exit corner of the mall. I caught up with him as we went through the exit door. Now I had a problem.

He had taken the back exit of the mall, which was where all of the huge trucks came in and out with supplies for the stores. I ran in one direction; he ran the other way. Trying not to get hit by the trucks was slowing me down, ruining my chance to catch him.

I saw the truck on the right getting ready to move out. If I wanted to catch him, I had to slow him down by shooting him in the leg. The truck was about to cut me off. I ran faster. When the truck was right in front of me, I rolled under it and took a shot. Bull's-eye.

I heard him scream in pain. When I got up, he was on the ground, holding his right, bleeding leg. Eli and Knuckles charged up. They heaved Don Franko to his feet and put him in handcuffs.

"You know Don Franko," I said as I walked up to him. I

showed him my bloody burn. "Do something like that again and I'll shoot you in both legs so that you won't be able to walk anymore."

"Ooo, a little girl is threatening me," he said sarcastically.

"You should feel threatened!" Commander Lino strode up. Commander Lino is our prime leader of the Royal Guards and somebody that you don't want to mess with. He was a military teacher for twenty years and then joined the top Royal Guards. Before my friends and I joined the Royal Guards, Commander Lino thought women were weak and that they should just stick to women's work. Thanks to me, not only did I prove that a girl could do anything a boy could do, but we could also do it while wearing high heels. Even though Commander Lino acts like a tough, strong, macho guy, deep down he has a soft side, too.

"She could have done a lot worse to you!" He sneered at Don Franko. "*But unlike the boys*, Layla knows the rules!" It took awhile for Eli and Knuckles to get it.

"Hey!" Eli and Knuckles glowered. I laughed at them.

All I can say about Eli and Knuckles is that they're all brawn and no brain, especially Knuckles. At least Eli has learned to think before he acts. Sometimes. Eli is one of those guys who likes to take it easy and have fun all the time. Whenever something bad happens, he always looks at the positive side of things. Knuckles, on the other hand, just likes to flirt around with the girls and show how tough he is (which he is). When Knuckles was a baby, he punched a wall and put a hole in it with his knuckles. That is why his parents called him Knuckles. Well, that's what they nicknamed him anyway. He won't tell us his real name. I figure that's because it's so embarrassing we'd never look at him as the same old tough guy ever again.

"Where's Sheena?" Fists on his hips, Commander Lino looked around.

"Probably still at the mall wiping the ketchup off her face," Eli told him as Knuckles laughed.

"Right, Eli, Knuckles!" Commander Lino nodded. "Take Don Franko to jail and explain the rules to him!"

"Yes sir," said Eli and Knuckles. They walked away with Don Franko between them. Eli turned around and waved. "See you at the wedding Layla!" Eli called.

"The wedding." I gulped. "I almost forgot."

"Well you better hurry, soldier!" snapped Commander Lino. "The wedding is in half an hour!"

"Right," I called back to Commander Lino as I ran off. "Bye!"

"Goodbye Layla!" Commander Lino yelled after me.

I ran to the church as quickly as I could. I knew I was going to make it. I just hoped that Princess Rose hadn't noticed that I was missing.

— Chapter Two —

The Wedding

Inside the church, I peeked around the corner. The coast was clear. I quickly ran into the dressing room. Closing the door behind me, I leaned on it and sighed in relief. No one had seen me sneak out and come back.

"So how was the chase?" asked a voice. "Did you catch Don Franko?" I opened my eyes to see Princess Rose in front of me. She had her arms crossed, and didn't look very happy with me.

"It took longer to catch him than I thought it would," I said, hoping it would make the princess laugh. I grabbed my maid of honour dress and slipped into the changing room.

"That's not funny, Layla." Rose wasn't amused. "Today's my wedding day and I told you not to go on the Don Franko mission."

"Oh come on Rose," I begged. "I had to take this mission. I'm getting so close to beating Eli and Knuckles to become the next Commander for the Royal Guards." Coming out of the changing room, I sat in front of the mirror to do up my hair and put on makeup. I don't like to wear makeup. It feels like I'm carrying dead weight on my face. But for Rose's special day, I decided that it couldn't hurt to wear makeup for one day. "If I become the next Royal Guard Commander, then that means ...."

"I know, I know," Rose said as she helped me fix my hair. "You'll become the first women to be in command."

"Right," I said.

"Come on Layla," said Rose, "You know you've already got the job." That was Princess Rose for you. Rose was the kindest and shyest person you'll ever meet. Just don't get on her bad side because if you do, she has a royal punishment for you.

I remember when I first met Rose. I was six years old and she was eight. I was dancing around in the forest when I heard someone crying in the bushes. I looked through the leaves and there she was. Sitting down, covering her face as she cried.

"Why are you crying?" I asked her. She jumped really high. I don't think she was expecting anyone to be around.

"Oh, well." She hesitated. "I'm crying because I can't remember the rules of being a princess."

"Wow, you're a princess?" I asked. I was pretty excited.

"Yes, I am," she said with no fear now. "I am Princess Rose of Jurassic."

"Well my name's Layla," I told her, "and I'm from Jurassic too."

"Wow that's great," said Rose joyfully. Then Rose put her head down, looking guilty. "Oh, I forgot the first rule of being a princess." I grabbed her right arm to stop her from going anywhere.

"You know Princess," I said softly, "I have a solution to help you remember your princess rules so that you'll never forget them."

"Really!" Rose beamed. "What is it?"

"Well when you're having trouble with something," I said, "all you have to do is relax and have some fun."

"I don't know," she said nervously. "My parents say that a princess has no time for fun."

"Trust me, Princess Rose," I said, grasping her hand. "You'll remember your rules if you have some fun." I pulled her out of the bushes. "Now come dance with me." I started to dance. Rose stood there for a while, obviously not sure what she should do. But then she started to move her feet and dance. We kicked our legs in the air, swung our arms from left to right, and spun in circles. Finally, we stopped dancing and sat down to catch our breaths.

"That was fun," she panted. "And I'm starting to remember the rules again." Then she hugged me so hard I thought I was going to pop like a balloon. "Thank you so much Layla!" I hugged her back.

"No problem. Princess Rose," I said. "After all, what are friends for?"

"Then as my best friend," she smiled, "you can just call me Rose."

"As you wish, Rose," I said. We laughed as we hugged. From that day forward, we've been best friends.

"Princess Rose, the wedding is about to start." Amy, one of our youngest members of the Royal Guards stuck her reddish brown-hair head in the door.

"We're ready," Rose told her. Amy smiled and shut the door.

Amy, how do I explain Amy? In three words: *love, psycho,* and *brat.* If you're a boy, then be careful how you talk to her. Look her in the eye even once and she thinks you're hers. And the more you push her away, the more she wants you. Her daddy makes sure she's happy and gets anything she wants. Now I don't care if Amy wastes her time over a guy she'll never get. I just don't like the fact that she's only thirteen years old and she's already looking for love and marriage.

We were all in our lines; Amy was in front with Sheena and Eli behind her, while Knuckles and I were behind them.

Sheena is the kind of person that likes to dream, talk, and hope that her wishes come true. Sheena never likes to be alone, especially when there are strangers around. You can't really blame her for not wanting to be alone though. Five years ago, before she came to Jurassic, she lived in a small country called Hope and Faith. Sheena was walking home when a strange man grabbed her and put her in his car. She was missing for three weeks. They found the man's secret hideout in a very creepy, swampy area. Sheena lost her left arm that day, which was replaced with a robotic arm.

"Oh Rose, darling." The King appeared at the doorway in his formal robes. "Shall we get this wedding going?"

"Yes we shall, Daddy," said Rose.

Once the music began playing, everyone marched down the aisle, couple by couple. When we were all in our position, the "Here Comes the Bride" song began to play. Rose and her father walked slowly down the aisle. Rose looked so beautiful in her dress. From her waist to the hem, the dress puffed out and she had a ribbon tied at the back of her waist. The top was strapless with an open back. Her face glowed with happiness. Her violet eyes sparkled and the lip-gloss that she wore made her light pink lips shine. On top of her short, rose pink hair, she wore a golden crown. When Princess Rose reached Prince Mark, the priest began to speak.

"Dearly beloved," said the priest, "we are gathered here today to unite Princess Rose with Prince Mark."

Yuck. I couldn't listen anymore. I couldn't stand Mark. None of us could. Prince Mark was just one of those annoying princes who thought he was the best and everyone should bow down to him. Prince Mark is the Prince of Snoflinga, a kingdom where it's always winter. When he first laid eyes on Rose, he asked her for her hand in marriage, but she couldn't stand him either, so she said no. He stalked her wherever she went. Every time Rose and I told him to get lost, he'd stay and always found a way to surprise us.

Every week or two, Prince Mark sent himself in a postal box to Vets Pets where Rose, Eli, and I volunteered to work for a day each week. Prince Mark's plan was that when Rose opened the box, he'd leap out and kiss her. Unfortunately, it was always Eli who opened the box. Poor Eli has been kissed so many times by Prince Mark that whenever Mark shows up, Eli hides behind Rose and me.

I noticed something on Prince Mark's face and took a closer look. Was that glitter on his face? And lips! Did I forget to mention that he was also totally into himself? Err, I don't know why Rose finally agreed to marry this creep.

"Do you, Princess Rose," said the priest, "take Prince Mark to be your husband?"

"I do," Rose said softly.

"And do you, Prince Mark," said the priest, "take Princess Rose to be your wife?"

"I absolutely do," said Prince Mark with pride.

Eww, even the way he said that made it sound so disgusting and cheesy.

"Then by the power invested by me," said the priest, "I now pronounce you husband and wife." Before the priest could finish saying, *you may now kiss the bride*, Rose and Prince Mark kissed.

— Chapter Three —

Announcement

"Boy, was that an awesome party or what?" asked the green-faced Knuckles as Eli and I tried to help him keep his balance.

"Yeah, it's really fun dragging you back to your home every time you gorge yourself at a party," said Eli sarcastically.

"And cleaning up the puke you leave behind," I added. I saw my Aunt Becky's house. I was only ten paces away from home.

"You can go home now Layla," Eli told me. I looked at him, shocked.

"Really?" I couldn't believe it. "Are you sure you don't want me to help you get Knuckles back home?"

"Don't worry." Eli smiled. "I'll get him home in no time."

"Okay then." I giggled and let go of Knuckles. Eli picked him up and slung him over his shoulders. "Come on Knuckles," said Eli. "Let's go home." As he walked away, he turned his head and waved at me. "See you tomorrow Layla!"

"Bye!" I shouted back.

I ran home and opened the door. Aunt Becky was in the kitchen washing dishes.

"Hello Dearie," Aunt Becky greeted me. "How was the party?"

"It was great," I said. "I'm going to bed now." I ran up the stairs.

"Layla, aren't you going to tell me about ...," said Aunt Becky. But I was already in my bedroom getting ready for bed. I put on my short, pink pyjama top, my green and pink striped pyjama bottoms, and jumped on my bed. I lay down and pulled up the blankets.

I really hope tomorrow comes soon. My eyes closed, I started to think about what had happened at the wedding party.

Everyone was talking, laughing, and having the time of their lives. Then Rose stood up, picked up her glass, and tapped the glass with her spoon.

"Attention everyone," Rose announced. "As the new Queen of Jurassic, I have a very important announcement to make." Everyone was quiet. "Now, I know the ceremony for the Royal Guards is tomorrow, but I'm sure Commander Lino wouldn't mind if I revealed who the next Commander is to be." Everyone stared at Commander Lino, waiting for his answer.

Commander Lino nodded and shouted, "Take it away your Highness."

Yes, the time to find out who was the next Commander of the Royal Guards was at hand. I looked back at Rose, nervous yet excited at the same time. I really hoped that I would be the next Commander. I wasn't the only candidate though. Knuckles was excited too.

Beyond this competition, if it really was a competition, Knuckles and I got along pretty well. Knuckles really wanted to be the next Commander, too. He wanted to prove that he was the smartest, bravest, and strongest person ever. Knuckles and I always compete and I always win. He hated that so much, mostly because he hates losing to a girl. The competition for being the next Commander was bringing out the bad side of our friendship.

"The next person to be Commander of the Royal Guards is a good friend of mine," said Rose. "In fact this person is a very close friend."

I'm a close friend to Rose. Heck, I was her best friend. I saw Knuckles glare at me with his violet eyes and clench his fists. I glared back at him and threw an air punch at him.

"This candidate worked so hard to earn this title," she continued. "This person has proved to be strong in battle, uses brains in a tough situation, and has risked his or her life several times." Suddenly someone opened the doors behind me and they slammed against the walls. It was Nilerm, the King and Queen's Personal Royal Assistant.

"Good evening your Highness." Nilerm bowed nervously to Rose.

"Nilerm, where have you been?" Rose looked furious.

"I'm so sorry your highness." He spread his hands. "But I had very important work to do."

"Fine, you may take your seat," said Rose. Nilerm walked to his seat while everyone gave him looks, especially me. Everyone probably thought he was telling the truth, but I knew better.

Nilerm was nothing but a schemer, a liar, a crazy man that always got himself into trouble. The only thing he did with his life was to try to take over the castle and become the King of Jurassic. I've stopped Nilerm many times. Rose tried to convince her parents to fire him from his position of assistant ruler. But because they don't like me for helping Rose be herself as a princess, they have refused. Nilerm was acting very strange though. When he got to his seat, he looked around as if somebody was watching him. I wonder what kind of trouble he has gotten into this time.

"Anyway," said Rose, "this person has done a lot of things to keep Jurassic a safe place." This was it. The moment of truth. "Which is why I'm glad to say that Layla Jenkins is the next Commander of the Royal Guards."

Yes, I'd done it. I was the first female ever to be Commander in Jurassic.

"Is there anything that you would like to say?" Rose asked me. I got out of my chair and stood up.

"Well I'd like to thank Commander Lino and Rose, I mean Her Highness, for making me the next Commander of the

Royal Guards," I said joyfully. "I would also like to thank my family and friends who believed in me. And as your next Commander, I'll do my best to protect Jurassic." Everyone clapped and cheered for me, everyone except for Knuckles.

He looked really mad and disappointed, as if he had been betrayed. It was going to take a while for Knuckles to accept the fact that I was the next Commander. But, he would eventually get over it and we'd be back to the kind of friends that annoyed each other. Knuckles clapped for me a little bit at the end. Eli ran over to me and put his arms over my shoulders.

"Now that that's over," Eli let go of me and turned to look at everyone, "let's get this party started!"

Everyone shouted in agreement and got to their feet. Either they went on the dance floor or they went right to the food and drinks.

I kept thinking and thinking about the wedding party until I finally started to slowly fall asleep.

— Chapter Four —

Under Attack

I heard a faint buzzing sound that slowly woke me. When I started to open my eyes, everything was a blur. The buzzing was getting louder.

"Buzz … Lay … buzz," I was hearing my walkie-talkie. I looked at my clock. My eyes finally focused. It was 3:00 a.m. in the morning. "Buzz … Layla … buzz." I got out of my bed and grabbed the walkie-talkie from my drawer. "Layla, come in," said a voice. It was Eli.

"Eli," I yawned.

"Layla get out!" Eli shrieked.

In a cranky mood now, I asked him, "Eli, why the heck are you calling me at 3 o'clock in the morning?"

"Layla, you have to get out of your house!" Eli sounded like he was freaking out.

"Out?" I asked. "Why do I have to get out of my house?"

"Because if you don't get out of the house you'll be trapped by a backhoe!" Eli screamed.

"A backhoe?" I stared at the walkie-talkie. Suddenly I felt my room shake and heard something rumbling outside. I climbed on my bed to look out the window. A dark yellow shadow was heading straight towards the house and it was opening grimy metal jaws.

"Layla look out!" Eli shrieked. I jumped off my bed as the wall of my bedroom was ripped off. I gasped. Half of the house

15

was gone. My bedroom, the kitchen, all gone.

It *was* a backhoe that had ripped out half of the house. But it wasn't the backhoe I was scared of. It was the person who was driving the backhoe: Nilerm. I stood there shocked, unable to move. What was Nilerm doing now?

I didn't snap out of it until I heard my young cousin Nikki's voice. "Layla, what's going on?"

"I don't know, but we have to get out of the house," I told her as I grabbed Nikki into my arms and ran down the stairs. When we were at least twenty-five feet away, Nikki and I watched Nilerm destroy the rest of our house.

"Layla, where's Mom?" Nikki clung to me, crying. I hugged her tightly.

"Don't worry Nikki, we'll find her," I said as I tried to calm her down.

But the only thing I could see around me was the destruction Nilerm was causing. Half of the buildings had crumbled to the ground and people were scrambling around the town trying to figure out where to go. I looked back at our torn up home, hoping that Aunt Becky was safe and sound.

"Layla!" shouted a faint voice. I turned around and saw that it was Eli. "Layla, are you okay?"

"I'm fine." I sighed and let Eli take Nikki. "I just need you to take Nikki to her mother while I stop Nilerm from destroying anything else."

"Right." Eli nodded. "I saw Becky just a minute ago, she's frantic about Nikki."

"Layla!" Nikki cried harder.

"Don't worry, Nikki," I said softly. "I'll be with you guys as soon as I stop Nilerm." Before Nikki could reply, Eli took off with her and they were gone.

"So Layla," shouted Nilerm. I turned around to look at Nilerm. He turned on the lights and turned the backhoe toward me, bathing me in their glare. "Shall we dance?"

"What do you think you're doing?" I yelled, not scared of him. He drove the backhoe toward me.

"That's for me to know." Nilerm raised the backhoe claw. "And for you to figure out!" The claw of the backhoe dove right down to trap me in it grasp. I dodged it just in time and ran, hoping Nilerm would follow me. "You can't get away this time, Layla!"

He fell for it. I had to get Nilerm away. Away from the people. Away from Jurassic. I had to get rid of him before he hurt anyone else. If I could lure Nilerm to drive to the main square of the Royal Guards' fighting arena there would be other Royal Guards to help me take him down. All of a sudden, I slammed into two people and fell to the ground. I got back up to see Knuckles and Amy on the ground.

"Amy, Knuckles," I yelled. "What are you two doing here? You should be helping the other Royal Guards to get people out of Jurassic."

"No way!" Knuckles screamed, "I'm not letting you take all the credit."

"Yeah," said Amy.

I pointed my finger at Amy in anger. "You need to go back to the other Royal Guards and help them out before you get yourself hurt!" I shouted. Then I looked over at Knuckles and pointed at him. "And how do you expect to fight with me when you're still puking up chunks like a cat coughing up a hairball?"

"Like this!" screamed Nilerm as the claw of the backhoe grabbed Knuckles, Amy, and me. I tried to get Amy and Knuckles out of the way, but it was too late. The claw had already trapped us and soil fell on us. Nilerm lifted the claw and started to speed up. As the soil surged around, I tried to push the upper joint of the claw open.

"Knuckles," I shouted, "I could use a little help here." Amy screamed but Knuckles just lay there.

"I'm busy here." He sounded relaxed.

"Help me out here!"

Knuckles mumbled something and got up. We both tried to push up the top to get out, but it was no use. We were trapped like rats. I punched up as hard as I could. "Oww!" I fell to my knees and held on to my numb, broken hand. "Dang it."

Amy was still screaming.

"Layla, are you alright?" Knuckles reached for my hand. I pulled it away and turned my back on him.

"I'm fine," I lied.

"I'd love to watch you die Layla," I heard Nilerm cackle, "but I have a kingdom to take over." I heard him jump off the machine, laughing, and run away. Hearing the word "die" made Amy scream even more loudly. Man, could that girl scream!

"Die?" Knuckles freaked. "What did he mean by die?" I was ready to give Knuckles a sarcastic answer when more soil slid down on us. The backhoe was tilting downward.

"Layla what's going on?" Amy screamed.

"We're falling off a cliff!" I yelled. "Hang on!" The backhoe stopped moving forward as gravity pulled us down. We all screamed. We fell back against the sides of the claw as the backhoe spun down. I felt like I was about ready to throw up. Screaming, we plunged to our doom.

— Chapter Five —

The Note

Opening my eyes gradually, I could barely make out the walls of the claw. It was dark. Amy and Knuckles were lying at my side. We were nearly buried in soil, and I couldn't believe I was still alive. I tried to get out of the soil as fast as I could. With my back stinging and my left hand broken, it was slow. Once I got the soil off me, I crawled over to Knuckles and Amy to see if they were still alive.

"Amy, Knuckles," I spoke softly. "Are you two alright?"

"Ugh, what happened?" Knuckles moaned.

"Knuckles!" I cheered as I hugged him one handed. "Thank goodness, you're alive."

"Ouch!" hissed Knuckles.

"Oops," I said as I let him go. "Sorry."

Knuckles looked around. "Are we dead?"

"No, we're still alive," I told him.

"What?" Knuckles sounded shocked. "I thought we fell off a cliff."

"We did," I said. "I'm just glad we survived. I don't know how, but at least we did." Then Knuckles and I heard Amy moaning. "Amy?" No response. I crawled over to her and dug her out of the soil. "Amy, can you hear me?" She still didn't respond. I grabbed her arm and checked her wrist. Yes, there was a pulse, but it wasn't very strong.

"How's Amy?" Knuckles asked.

"She still has a pulse," I said, "but it's just barely there. We have to get her to a hospital and fast."

"Right," said Knuckles confidently. But when he tried to stand up, he hit his head on the claw of the backhoe. "Ouch!" He fell back down. I closed my eyes, put my hand on my forehead, and shook my head in disbelief. Then I opened my eyes and saw light. "Knuckles do you see that?"

He looked around. "Yeah I do see it."

"Which means we found our way out of here," I said gladly. "Now dig us out of here Knuckles."

"What," Knuckles said in annoyance. "Why do I have to do all the digging?"

"Because not only are you our fastest digger," I explained to him, "but Amy can't do anything and I'm no help with a broken hand."

"Fine," complained Knuckles. While Knuckles was digging, I stood partly up to see how my back was. The pain was fading. But the pain in my hand wasn't gone. I held on to my hand for support. Then suddenly I felt dirt on my back.

"Hey!" I said, "Watch where you're throwing the dirt."

"There, all done," said Knuckles, proud of himself. He looked at me. "Now let's get out of here."

I pulled Amy to Knuckles. He pulled her through the pit and to the outside. Then he grabbed my good hand and pulled me into the pit and through to the outside. I couldn't believe what I was seeing; it was like a desert—a dry land full of rocks and sand. The sky was clear. No clouds, but I couldn't see the sun. When I looked behind me, I saw huge mountains. There was no telling their width, they seemed to stretch on forever. *Where had we fallen from?* I felt a cold chill. What had Nilerm done? Where had he sent us?

"Okay." Knuckles was starting to freak out. "This is getting weirder and weirder." I looked to the left.

"Knuckles look." I pointed with my good hand. "There's a car over there." We ran over to the car. Knuckles put Amy in the back seat and tried to start it. Nothing happened.

"Well we're not getting anywhere by car," Knuckles growled. I found a bag in the back and unzipped it. Inside the bag were tons of different clothes. "Whoa, check out the clothes." I held out one of the garments. It was really beautiful, too, made of doeskin—the fake kind though, not the real kind. It had one thick strap on the left side and it slid down to the right. On the bottom, it was trimmed with bits of fur. It completely covered your butt to your knees.

"Wow," Knuckles said amazed, "Look at all of them." While he looked at the clothes, I went around to the front of the car. There were the usual seatbelts, comfy seats, radio, air conditioner, and then the glove box that was always on the right side. I opened the glove box, finding a note with a red and blue feather inside.

"Well what do we have here?" I said curiously. I walked over to Knuckles. "Hey Knuckles, look what I found,"

"A note," said Knuckles curiously too. "What's it say?"

"*Dear Overlanders,*" I started to read.

"Overlanders?" Knuckles said in confusion.

I kept reading. "*If you are reading this, then it means you're in a world full of danger.*"

"Couldn't they at least tell us what the dangers are?" complained Knuckles.

"Knuckles, be quiet," I snapped. "*There are so many things I have not seen before,*" I read on. "*Things that I would never even imagine.*" Knuckles and I gulped. "*In the back of the car, there are some clothes to help you blend in. But whatever clothes you choose to wear, be careful. It may mean the difference between life and death.*"

"Where the bloody heck are we?" Knuckles looked around. I held on to the doeskin garment I had admired and took out another dress for Amy.

"Cover me, okay?" I said as I put the red and blue feather in my hair.

"Wait, where are you going?" Knuckles shouted after me.

"I'm going back under the backhoe to change," I told him.

"Watch out for anyone coming," I yelled, "then I'll help Amy get into that dress." I went back under the backhoe to change. It was a bit tricky getting the dress on in the little space I had. But I managed to get it on with no trouble. When I came out, Knuckles looked at me, stunned.

"Wow, you look great." He nodded. The dress just barely went over my knees.

"Thanks Knuckles," I smiled. "Now turn your back so I can dress Amy." For once, he didn't argue and I pulled her dress on without a peek from him. "Now let's go."

"Huh?" Knuckles looked confused. "Where are we going?"

"To look for a village," I said. "The sooner we find a village, the sooner we'll find a doctor to help Amy, and figure out where we are."

"Right, I knew that," Knuckles lied. I rolled my eyes and walked. Knuckles grabbed Amy and followed me. We were on our way to find out where we were.

— Chapter Six —

A New World

"We've been walking for hours," Knuckles complained. "Can we at least take a break?"

"Fine," I said, "as soon as we find a water hole." We walked a bit more until we found a spring bubbling out from under a rock. Relieved, we ran over to the water, crouched down, and drank. I checked Amy's pulse again. Her heartbeat was a little stronger than last time, but it was still barely there. "Come on Knuckles," I said, "we have to keep going."

"Okay," Knuckles agreed. He carried Amy in his arms and we started walking again. "Do you think we'll find a village soon?"

"I don't know?" I answered. "But I sure hope so." As we were walking, some sort of black spherical thing flew right at us. "Whoa!" I shouted as I managed to dodge it. But it wrapped around Knuckles legs.

Knuckles yelled.

It was a shackle with two balls at each end that had tangled up his legs.

"Knuckles," I called as I went to help him. I felt two arms from behind pick me up. "What the ...?"

"Well what do we have here?" asked a man.

"It looks like we've got a couple of outcasts," said the other man. They sounded older than us, maybe twenty-five.

"You better let go of me or else ... " I threatened them as I looked up at them. They were really tall and buff. But that's not what freaked me out. I wasn't really sure what was freaking me out more; what they were going to do to us or that they were humanoid lizard men.

"What the heck are you?" Knuckles yelled.

"What's wrong, outcast?" asked the lizard man on my left.

"You look like you've seen a ghost." The lizard man on my right snickered. Thinking quickly, I kicked one in the shins and went to punch the other. He dodged and punched me.

I shrieked and fell to the ground hard. My eyesight went blurry and grew darker until it was pitch black. Then everything started to come back. My eyesight was back to normal but I was in a different place, in a wooden carriage of some sort. On my right, I saw bars that locked us up like prisoners.

"Layla," said Knuckles, relieved, "thank goodness you're alright."

"Knuckles?" I looked around. "What's going on?" Then I realized I was putting pressure on my left hand and it didn't hurt. I looked at my hand and saw that it was covered in green bandages. "What did they do to my hand?"

"You were unconscious," explained Knuckles, "and while you were, they fixed your hand up."

"Oh," I said, shocked. "Well, that was nice of them."

"I don't think so." Knuckles frowned. "They're taking us to their village."

"What's so bad about that?" I asked.

"They're taking us there to punish us." Knuckles sounded serious. "Apparently they don't like outcasts."

"Well if they don't like outcasts, what will they think of Overlanders?" I glanced over to Amy. "Oh my gosh, is Amy alright?"

"Don't worry, she's fine," said Knuckles, trying to calm me. "They helped get her pulse back to normal."

"If she's fine then why isn't she awake?"

Knuckles thought about it for a moment, then shrugged his

shoulders. "I don't know. They just said something about Amy being in a comma."

"That's coma, you fool." I rolled my eyes.

"Oy, be quiet," hissed one of the lizard man.

"Yeah, we're almost at our destination," said the other lizard man.

Knuckles and I tried to look through the small window in the front seat, but the lizard men's heads were in our way. So we just looked through the bars that locked us up. I heard both the lizard men talking to other people about getting the gate open. Then I heard the doors creeping open slowly, opening to a new world.

— Chapter Seven —

That's Not Our Names

Inside the fort, everything changed. There was no more dry sand and dirt. It had been replaced by cement. Houses and shops were all close together. But the people were even stranger. Not only were there regular humans like us, with normal skin, but there were some who had blue, red, green, yellow, orange, or even purple skin. Some of them weren't even humans. In fact, most of them were humanoid animal mixes: dogs, cats, lizards, foxes, wolves, you name it. They looked at us as if we were the monsters. The carriage stopped moving.

"Yo, Drake boy!" called one of the lizard men. Knuckles mouthed the words *Drake boy* to me.

"Open the inner gate!" said the other one. We heard the gate open and the carriage moved again.

"Where are we going?" grumbled Knuckles.

"I don't know," I told him, "ask the lizards."

When the gates closed, I looked back and saw the cemented walls. There were guards on top wearing armour. They had bows and arrows in their hands. The whole thing looked like the entrance to a castle. Oh my gosh, we were inside a castle. The carriage stopped moving again. The two lizard men opened the gate and grabbed Knuckles and me.

"Come on now, outcasts," said the lizard man that had grabbed Knuckles.

"Lady Katherine and Sir Roger would like to see you," said the lizard man that grabbed me.

"Wait a min!" I tried to pull free. "What about our friend?"

"Don't worry," said the one still holding on to me, "we've got people to look after her."

Some people hurried up and took Amy with them. Wow, this castle was huge.

They took us up a couple of stairways in those tall towers. My heart was racing. I had no idea what was going on and I really didn't want to find out. The two lizard men looked like identical twins. They both had purple skin and mullet haircuts. All business in the front, party in the back. They had normal lizard noses, but their eyes were bizarre. They were glowing red and they had no pupils. We were outside at the top of the castle. There were bushes and a huge pool with a diving board. Wait, pool, diving board? What was a pool and diving board doing inside a castle?

I saw Knuckles trying to struggle out of the lizard men's grip. I just let the reptiles take me were they wanted because I knew trying to struggle wasn't going to get me anywhere. As Commander Lino told us, *It doesn't matter what size you are, you can get out of anyone's grip. You just have to wait for the right time.* Knuckles was getting ticked off.

"Yo, lizard freaks!" Knuckles shouted. The lizard man holding him punched him in the stomach.

"That's not our names," said the lizard man in anger.

"What are your names then?" I asked kindly. If I played the innocent nice card, they wouldn't expect anything from me, especially the fact that I could kick their butts. They looked at me strangely for a while but then they smiled at me.

"Well my name's Flax," said the lizard man holding on to Knuckles.

"And I'm Granate," said the one holding on to me.

"Well Flax and Granate," I said, "I hope you don't mind me asking, but who are Lady Katherine and Sir Roger?"

"They're your guardian teachers," said Granate.

"Guardian teachers?" I asked.

"Yeah, they'll be teaching and training you on how to take care of yourselves the proper way," said Flax, "while they protect you from the danger around here."

"Danger!" Knuckles' eyes got wide. "Can't we just go back to our homes where it's safe for us?" Flax and Granate laughed.

"No way." Granate giggled. "Once you're here, you stay here.

"Whether you like it or not." Flax chuckled.

Once they stopped laughing, I asked them a bit more harshly now, "Has any outcast tried to escape?"

Flax and Granate looked at each other. Then they looked at me and said, "Nope."

"Well then," I said getting ready to strike, "I guess there's a first for everything." With that said, I kicked Granate in the guts, grabbed his neck, and threw him at Flax. Flax let go of Knuckles when Granate hit him and they both banged into the wall.

"Come on Knuckles, let's go." We bolted for it. It didn't take long though for Granite and Flax to get back up.

"Oy, come back here!" I heard Flax shout as they chased us.

"Great, now what?" Knuckles asked.

"Split up and meet each other outside," I ordered. Knuckles went left with Flax following him while I went right with Granate following me.

— Chapter Eight —

Sora and Soda

With my big lead on Granate, I had to find a hiding place quick. I turned right and saw a row of suits of armour standing along each side of the hall. Running half way up the hall, I hid behind one of the suits. Suddenly Granate came around the corner then stopped. He walked slowly, looking to each side. My heart was racing but steady at the same time. Then Granate looked in my direction and I froze. His suspicious eyes searched as he came closer and closer. I closed my eyes and shivered, wishing he were somewhere else. But before he reached me, a voice called out, "Granate!"

I opened my eyes as Granate turned around.

"Oh, hey Flax," Granate greeted him, "where did the red-haired outcast go?"

"Dealing with the Dark Prince." Flax's eyes gleamed.

"Ooo, that boy's in trouble now," laughed Granate as they walked away.

"Wait till I tell you what he did to get himself in trouble," said Flax.

"What did he do, what did he do?" I heard Granate begging in a fading voice.

I peeked out to make sure that they were gone. Great, now I had to go save Knuckles as usual. I ran off, looking behind me to see if anyone was following me, which was the wrong thing to do because I slammed into two guys.

We all yelped and hit the ground. I sat up, holding my head.

"Oh my gosh," I said feeling horrible, "I'm so sorry."

They sat up as well and looked at me strangely. They were two teenage boys with brightly colored spiked hair, but probably a year older than I was. Then they laughed. What was so funny?

"There's no need to apologize," said the boy with the sky blue spiked hair.

"Especially a pretty girl like you." The boy with the lime green spiked hair was flirting. I rolled my eyes at him.

"How many times have you used that line?" I asked sarcastically. His smirk turned into an angry frown.

"Apparently too many," laughed the blue spiked boy. He grabbed my hand and we both stood up. "My name's Sora and this is my second twin brother Soda."

"Second twin?" I asked confused.

"Yeah, we're actually triplets," said Soda, "but our other brother isn't here."

"Wow," I said, amazed, "fraternal triplets."

"Yeah," Sora said awkwardly. "That's a pretty big word for an outcast to know."

Crap. "Well ... uhh ...," I stammered trying to think of something quickly.

"So she's smarter than some of the other outcasts," said Soda. "Big deal, in fact ..." he grabbed my hand as he used his other hand to touch my arm. "I find it attractive when a girl is smarter than me."

"Oh really?" I said teasing him. "Well how do you feel about a girl that's stronger than you?" Before he could answer, I held on to his hand and twisted his arm behind his back.

Soda yelled and fell to the ground holding on to his arm, and all Sora could do was point at him and laugh.

"Man, I like you!" Sora cried laughing. When he caught his breath, he looked at me, and asked, "What's your name?"

"It's Layla," I told him. "Layla Jenkins."

"Sweet name," said Sora giving me the thumbs up. "Follow me."

As Sora and I walked off, Soda jumped up and caught up to us. They were definitely fraternal twins. Besides having different hair colours, Sora had emerald, green eyes while Soda had sky blue eyes. Sora had a little mole on his right shoulder while Soda had a big, weird, permanent looking scar in the shape of the letter "S." Even though they were fraternal twins, they did have some similarities. Same height, same strong but boyish body shape, and the same long, spiked back hair. Neither had a shirt on, but they wore very baggy pants. I wondered what the third twin looked like.

"So where are we going?" I asked curiously.

"Our third twin brother, Shaine, is punishing an outcast," explained Sora.

"Yeah, some red haired idiot was flirting with his fiancé," Soda added.

"That's horrible," I said feeling terrible. Oh, please tell me that wasn't *my* red haired idiot.

"Here we are," said Sora.

He opened the doors and walked in. This had to be the biggest throne room I had ever seen. There were thousands of people inside laughing and having a good time. I stuck close to them both, especially Sora.

"So," I said, "which one is the girl that's marrying your brother Shaine?" He looked around trying to find her.

"Ah, there she is." Sora smiled and pointed to her. "Sitting on that chair over there." I took couple of steps to get a closer look at the girl.

"Whoa," I said stunned.

She was really beautiful. She had short, half-curled, white hair, gleaming blue eyes and fair skin. Oh yeah, she was definitely Knuckles' type.

"Yup, Shaine is marrying the most beautiful girl ever." Soda sounded annoyed. Then he looked at me and smiled. "Besides you, though."

"Alright, cut it out Soda," said Sora as he pushed Soda away from me a bit. "Her name is Sylvia. She's the brattiest princess you'll ever meet."

"Princess?" I was surprised. "But if she's a princess and marrying your brother, then that makes you ..." I gasped at the thought of it. "Oh my gosh, I'm so sorry for not knowing you two were royalty, Prince Sora."

I started to bow to them both but Prince Sora stopped me. "Please Layla, there's nothing to forgive," said Prince Sora. "As our new special friend, just call us by our first names okay?"

"Thank you," I said.

"Anyway," Sora continued to talk, "Sylvia is a bratty princess who thinks she's the most gorgeous girl on this whole planet."

"Good to know." I smiled. This was great. There was no way then she would give Knuckles the time of day. I looked around the place.

"Wow, this place is so huge you could have a battle here," I joked.

"Well this throne room is part of a battle field," said Soda.

"What?" I was shocked.

"You didn't think the Dark Prince was just going to sit on his throne and discuss what the outcast's punishment would be did you?" Soda laughed quietly.

"D ... Dark Prince?" I stuttered.

"Yeah, our brother isn't really what you call a 'good boy'," Sora explained.

"And he likes to deal with his rivals by having a fight with them," Soda added, trying to scare me.

"Boy, that is pretty bad." Suddenly everyone was quiet and looking at the doors.

"Well Layla," said Sora, "you're about to see your first battle."

I looked at the doors too, as they opened. I wasn't happy with what I saw as Flax and Granate came in holding Knuckles between them.

— Chapter Nine —

Fight to the Finish

Knuckles was struggling to get out of Flax's and Granate's grip. Everyone looked back at the king and queen's throne. Someone was coming from behind them.

"There's our brother, Shaine," Sora whispered. There was only one word I could use to describe their brother—*Wow*!

Not only was Shaine, uhh I mean Prince Shaine, completely different from Sora and Soda, but he was really good looking. I mean there are a lot of attractive men, but he had his own sort of glow about him. He had really short, slicked down, black hair with one red streak. Wearing no shirt, you could see how ripped he was. He definitely had more muscle than Sora and Soda, but he wasn't over the top muscled like Commander Lino, or Flax and Granate. But what made him stand out the most were his eyes. They were crimson.

"All hail the Dark Prince!" shouted Flax and Granate. I bowed to the ground like everyone else. Knuckles refused to bow, but Flax and Granate pushed him down. Prince Shaine was very angry and upset, while Princess Sylvia looked worried.

"Your name, outcast?" Prince Shaine asked coldly.

"The name's Knuckles," said Knuckles. "But you can just call me Knucklehead."

Oh Knuckles you idiot. Prince Shaine looked at him like he, too, knew that Knuckles was an idiot. He walked towards him.

"Do you know why you're here?" Prince Shaine asked in anger.

"I was hoping you could tell me so that we could get this over with," said Knuckles being a smart-aleck. Granate punched Knuckles in the stomach and Knuckles choked.

"No back talk to the Dark Prince!" snapped Flax. Prince Shaine stopped walking and glared at the prisoner.

"You are here because you were flirting with my fiancé," said Prince Shaine, even angrier now. "And for your punishment, we will fight to the finish."

Knuckles smiled. "Hah, bring it on. I'm gonna beat you up so much that you'll be crying for your mommy."

I rolled my eyes and smacked my hand on my forehead. Knuckles thought that fight to the finish meant you fight until someone surrendered. I always had to tell him that fight to the finish meant you fight until someone dies. The Dark Prince smiled.

"Let him go, guards," Prince Shaine ordered. Flax and Granate let go of Knuckles. He stretched out his muscles while Prince Shaine just stood there waiting impatiently.

"Uhh, Sora," I whispered, "just out of curiosity, how many people have beaten your brother?"

"Honestly?" Sora whispered. Suddenly, Prince Shaine slammed Knuckles into a wall. "None."

Gasping, I watched Prince Shaine punch Knuckles repeatedly. Knuckles managed to dodge one of his punches and then punched the prince up into the air. Prince Shaine grabbed Knuckles and choked him from behind. I looked over to Princess Sylvia and saw how scared she was as she watched this happening. Knuckles struggled for air. Luckily, though, he remembered Commander Lino's strategy. Knuckles elbowed the prince in the stomach, grabbed his arms, and threw him across the room. Prince Shaine slid across the floor. He got back up but used his right arm to hold on to his left side.

"Impressive," admitted Prince Shaine. "You're stronger than I thought."

"Heh, it takes a lot to bring me down," said Knuckles.

"Well then," said Prince Shaine, "let's make the game harder."

Then he suddenly disappeared. I gasped in shock. How was that even possible? I could see that Knuckles was starting to get nervous as he looked around to find the prince. He reappeared behind Knuckles and punched him in the back. Knuckles quickly got back up on his feet and started to punch the Dark Prince, but he had already vanished. He kept disappearing and reappearing to whack Knuckles. He managed to get a couple of hits on the prince, but it wasn't enough to bring the prince down. Finally, Knuckles was on the ground bleeding from head to toe. I had to think of something fast. If I interfered with the battle, we'd both be dead. But if I didn't do anything, Knuckles would be dead, leaving me on my own.

Quickly I turned to Sora, "Is there anything we can do to stop this?"

Sora looked at me like that was a very strange question to ask but he thought about it. "Well," he finally whispered, "the only way you can win with Shaine is with a very good argument." A good argument. No problem. But how was I going to do it?

Suddenly I heard everyone, except for Sora, scream, "Kill, kill, kill!" Prince Shaine was slowly walking towards Knuckles with a knife in his hand. I could hear Princess Sylvia crying now. He stopped in front of Knuckles.

"Wait, I didn't think we were going to kill each other!" cried Knuckles.

"That's what 'fight to the finish' means, you fool!" Prince Shaine explained with pleasure. He brought his knife down.

"No!" I screamed as I ran towards them. Everyone gasped and whispered to each other. I looked up at Prince Shaine. He looked so surprised as I stood over Knuckles. I think it was the first time that someone had actually interfered in one of his battles.

"Please don't kill him, he didn't know any better," I begged. The Dark Prince and I both knew that was a lie. Everyone was looking at us, waiting for the Dark Prince's command. He just stood there, silently watching us. Sora and Soda looked nervous for me.

"I know what he did was wrong, but I'll make sure he doesn't go near your fiancé ever again."

Prince Shaine closed his eyes, thinking. Knuckles' blood dripped into the dust and he was breathing heavily. My heart was beating fast. The prince was shaking the knife. He was going to kill us. My argument wasn't good enough. I put my head down and closed my eyes. Then suddenly, I heard something drop to the ground. It was the Dark Prince's knife. Everyone went quiet when Prince Shaine turned around and dropped his knife. He turned to face me and opened his eyes.

"If you can keep that promise then he'll live," Prince Shaine told me, "but if you don't, then you both die." And he walked away.

— Chapter Ten —

Owashia

I couldn't believe what just happened. Did I really just change the Dark Prince's mind? I was so shocked at what had happened that Granate had to carry me out of the throne room. I didn't know where Flax and Granate were taking Knuckles and me, but I didn't care. I couldn't stop thinking about what had just happened. I couldn't stop thinking about him. The way Prince Shaine talked. The way he acted. The way he had looked at me. It was all too weird. The sound of his voice and actions might have been those of a Dark Prince, but not his eyes. Behind those crimson eyes, I saw a kind heart and soul but he had to hide himself. He didn't want to hide anymore. What was I saying? I barely knew the guy and I was already talking about how sweet and caring he was and how he was too shy to show himself to the world.

Shaking my head to bring myself back to reality, I looked at Granate and Flax. "Where are you taking us?"

"Well right now we're kicking your friend here into Sir Rogers' training room," replied Flax as he shoved Knuckles into the room.

"Ouch!" shouted Knuckles. He turned around to face Flax. "My name's Knuckles, you big fat ... !" Before he could finish his sentence, Flax shut and locked the door on him.

"And we're taking you to Lady Katherine's room," Granate smiled as we all continued to walk, "where she will teach you how to be a lady."

"Sorry to disappoint," I told them, "but I already took that class and I passed with flying colours."

"You're lying," snapped Flax.

"I'm telling you the truth," I said innocently. But they just glared at me with disbelief. I glared back at them. "Fine, if you don't believe me then look at my ID profile. It'll tell you everything."

Flax and Granate gave me a weird look. They gave me the same look that Sora had given me when I said fraternal triplets.

"That's the first time I've ever heard an outcast tell us to look at their ID profile," said Flax suspiciously.

Crap, I did it again.

"So what do we do?" asked Granate before I could say anything. Flax scratched his head, not really sure what to do either.

"Well," said Flax trying to think, "we could go check her ID profile and see if she speaks the truth."

"Okay," Granate agreed. "What's your name, love?"

"Layla," I said.

"And your last name?" Flax asked in a grumpy tone.

"Jenkins," I said.

"Well it's nice to meet you Layla Jenkins." Granate smirked.

"Don't talk to her," said Flax in anger. "She could be tricking us so then she can beat us up and run away again."

"Right, I knew that." Granate sounded embarrassed. I couldn't help but giggle at them a little.

Flax and Granate were complete opposites yet they couldn't be better friends. Flax seemed to be a grumpy lizard who liked to make fun of outcasts and didn't like to make a fool of himself on his job. Granate, on the other hand, was a sweet, humble guy who was always happy and got distracted at times during his job. The only thing they had in common was that they weren't the brightest lizard people. Then again, they were the only lizard people I've met.

"Here we are," said Flax. It was a fair sized room. On the left side of the room, there was a sandy, brown couch with a plant on a table to the left. In front of me was a huge computer. Wait, they have a computer down here?

"This just keeps getting weirder by the minute," I mumbled.

"Sit," ordered Flax harshly. I sat on the couch while Flax and Granate went onto the computer to search for my ID profile.

"What is this place?" I asked.

"The information room," replied Granate.

"It's where we get all of our information," explained Flax, "from looking at an ID profile, to spying on our enemies."

"Really?" I watched as they entered my name in the computer. "Even people called Overlanders?" Flax turned around and gave me an angry look.

"Sadly no," Flax answered. The computer was still searching. It was taking a long time for the computer to find my profile. I thought I was going to fall asleep.

"Is this the only computer you have?" I yawned.

"No, there is one more computer around," Granate answered.

"Really?" I was interested.

"Yeah, but it belongs to the Dark Prince," Flax pointed out. "So don't even think about sneaking into his computer room. You'll get caught and he'll give you a dreadful punishment." I rolled my eyes. I've snuck into thousands of secret computer rooms, whether in training or spying on somebody like Nilerm, and have never been caught. This was just another challenge for me.

"So how come you guys don't call the Dark Prince by his first name?" I asked.

"Because it's forbidden to call him by his first name," answered Granate, "unless you have permission from him."

"Is he really that evil?" I wanted the truth.

"That's also forbidden to answer," Flax added. "What's with all the questions about him?" I blinked at Flax's question.

"Well … I don't know," I told him. "He … just seems … different that's all."

"Here it is," said Granate, all happy. "Layla Jenkins and

according to her ID profile, she has already graduated from Becoming a Lady." Flax made his grumpy noise.

"What's wrong Flax?" I smirked at him. "Were you hoping that I was lying?"

"You know for someone who has graduated from Becoming a Lady," Flax smirked at me now, "you don't really act like a lady."

"Well the first rule of becoming a lady is that you must always be yourself," I said, "no matter how unladylike you may be at times."

"Ooo, you really are a lady," said Granate trying to compliment me.

"Uhh, thanks Granate," was all I could say to him. How could they have access to my ID profile? Especially when Flax had said that they couldn't get any information about Overlanders on this computer. It was clear that this was not my real ID profile. But who would make a fake one for me? And why? Could the Dark Prince be behind this? Flax also said that he had his own computer. I'll have to find some more information on the Dark Prince when Flax and Granate are gone. For now, I was safe. "So now what?"

"Right, well," said Flax as we walked out of the information room, "look for a job and enjoy the rest of your life at Owashia."

"Owashia?" I asked, a bit confused.

"Yeah, this is what the town is called," said Granate, "Owashia."

While Flax and Granate went one way, I walked in the opposite direction. Time to look for some answers.

— Chapter Eleven —

The Library

I explored the cold stone castle to see what I could find. The only thing I found though were a bunch of bedrooms. Nothing else. Then I saw a silver metal door. I went up to it and turned the knob. It was locked. It was strange because all the other rooms in the castle were unlocked. What was in this room that they had to have it locked up? Deciding to investigate it later, I continued on my search to find some information.

Ten minutes later, I saw huge doors that said *Library* at the top.

"Perfect," I said with joy. When I opened the doors, I was amazed at how huge it was. There were two levels with a staircase on each side. And of course, there were tons of books. I went to the front counter to ask a question but no one was there.

"Huh," I sighed. "Guess I'll have to find the book I want myself." I sat on the chair to examine the Index of Books.

"This is a very big book," I said, amazed. I opened the book and dust flew everywhere.

"And apparently it hasn't been used in awhile." I coughed as I tried to fan the dust away. "Let's see." I ran my finger down the list of books that started with O. "Overboard, Over the Hedge, Over the hill … Aha, Overlanders. Bottom level, left side in the O section, book code DKL."

I closed the book and walked over to the O bookshelf. I climbed up the ladder and pushed myself over to the DKL section. I moved my fingers over the books until I found the Overlanders book.

"Ahh, here it is." I grabbed the book and flipped the pages. "Wow, this isn't a very big book."

I went down the ladder then over to one of the library tables and sat down. I opened the book and read the first page. *What is an Overlander? An Overlander is a person that lives on the top side of Dysnomia.*

"Top side!" I whispered, hoping no one else was in here to hear that. I continued reading silently.

Overlanders are nothing but rich and greedy people that would do anything to get power in their hands. They don't care about anyone but themselves. Overlanders are not the kind of people you can trust, because they can't even trust themselves. If you came up to their world, they would judge you on the spot and torment you for being different. Maybe even kill you. Overlanders know nothing of this world and it should always be that way.

I resented all of this. Sure, there might be some people like that, but there are also lots of kind-hearted people that live in my world. I turned over the next page and continued reading.

What do you do if you run into an Overlander? If you ever run into an Overlander, kill them.

I gasped. Nilerm had thrown me, Knuckles, and Amy into a secret underground world that would kill us on sight, the minute they found out we were Overlanders. I didn't get it. I mean I understand why Nilerm would want to get rid of me, but why Amy and Knuckles?

I grabbed the book, went quickly up the ladder, and put it back in its place. I sighed and leaned my head on the bar. Then I noticed a book that revealed the letters TH DA PRI. It stood for "The Dark Prince."

"Well, what do we have here?" I reached for the book when my foot slipped off the ladder.

I yelled as I fell, with my eyes closed.

I thought I was going to hit the floor, but someone caught me by the hips. Not sure whose shoulders I was holding on to, I opened my eyes and gasped. It was the Dark Prince, Shaine. He didn't look very happy, either. Eyes and mouth wide open, he let go of my hips and clasped my body against his chest. I felt my cheeks going red as I looked up at Prince Shaine.

"You alright?" Prince Shaine asked.

"Uhh ... yeah I'm ... I'm fine," I could barely speak. He put me down.

"What are you doing here?" Prince Shaine asked curiously.

"Oh I was reading a book about Overlanders," I answered.

"Overlanders?" He laughed, "Why is an outcast reading a book about Overlanders?"

"I was just curious ... about what your people know about Overlanders," I said. "I've never seen an Overlander."

"Interesting," said Prince Shaine. "Who are you?"

"Oh I'm ... I'm Layla ... Layla Jenkins," I stumbled.

"So you're Layla Jenkins," said Prince Shaine. "Follow me." He walked out of the library and I followed.

That was weird. Had he really forgotten who I was? It's not like I was wearing different clothes to confuse him.

"So," Prince Shaine spoke, "where's your knuckleheaded friend?"

"His name is Knuckles," I said walking beside him, "and he's exactly where he's supposed to be."

"Hmm," Prince Shaine frowned. "Well, we'll see how long that will last. Your other friend is in there." Prince Shaine pointed to a white door that had a red cross on the bottom and a circular window at the top, like hospital doors up in my world. "Talk to Doctor Beak. He'll tell you everything you need to know." I walked past him and opened the front door. As I was going inside, I turned around to thank him. But the Dark Prince was already gone. I blinked. Who was this guy?

— Chapter Twelve —

Dr. Beak

I waited for Dr. Beak. Everything was quiet in the room. The only thing you could hear was the ticking of the clock.

"Are you Layla Jenkins?" asked a doctor. I looked up and tried not to let my jaw drop. He was a duck. A yellow talking duck with a black eye patch on his left eye, an orange beak, and orange feet. He wore a white coat with a stethoscope around his neck.

"Yeah," I said nervously.

"Oh goody," quacked the doctor. "My name is Dr. Beak. Please follow me, Layla Jenkins."

"Umm, could you just call me Layla?" I followed him, even more nervous now.

"Very well then Layla," said Dr. Beak. "Do you know why you're here?"

"Yes, I do," I answered. "Is Amy going to make it?"

Dr. Beak laughed quietly. "It's just a coma, dearie." Dr. Beak quacked again as he reached to my cheek with his wing. Long feathers at the tips seemed to work like fingers.

Ahhh, he was pinching my cheek. I hated it when people pinched my cheeks. It made me feel like a little kid that no one listens to.

"She'll be out of it by tomorrow morning." Dr. Beak interrupted my thoughts.

I put my hand over my heart, relieved. Dr. Beak pulled the

curtains and I saw Amy lying in a bed. He gave me a key. "You can take her back to your room. It's on the second floor."

"Thank you Dr. Beak." I smiled.

"You're welcome," said Dr. Beak. Dr. Beak and I rolled Amy's bed out of the hospital room and into the waiting room. "Will you need any assistance?" he called after me.

"Oh no thank you, I'll be alright," I told him. With that said, I left the room. I looked at the key to see the number of my room. Room one hundred and fourteen. Suddenly someone hurried around the corner and bumped right into Amy's bed.

"Ouch," moaned Knuckles.

"Knuckles!" I shook him. "What are you doing?"

"Layla, I wasn't doing anything," Knuckles said nervously. "I was uhh …" He looked behind his back and pulled out a rose. "Picking out a flower for you."

Not buying any of it, I decided to play along.

"Oh really," I said pretending to flirt with him as I took the rose and sniffed it.

"Yeah, cause you're my girl," Knuckles lied. I glanced at the note attached to the rose.

"You know, it's kind of hard to believe this rose is for me," I said in anger. I showed him the note. "Because I don't remember my name ever being Sylvia!" Busted, he froze with fear.

"I see you're busy." Knuckles backed up, trying to make a quick getaway. I grabbed him by the arm and twisted it.

"Oh no you don't," I said furiously. "You're going to help me push Amy down to our room."

"Fine." Knuckles huffed and helped me push Amy's bed. When we were on the second floor, I found our room number and unlocked the door.

There were three beds. Two stood on the left and one big one stood on the right. In between the two beds, there was a small chest of drawers with a lamp on top. It also had a balcony with curtains hiding it.

"Not bad," I said cheerfully. I leaped onto the big bed while Knuckles wheeled in Amy and lifted her onto her bed.

"Well if that's all you need," said Knuckles trying to sneak off. I stepped in front of him.

"Nice try Knuckles." I grabbed him. "You're staying right here, and are not allowed to be around Princess Sylvia."

"Jealous much?" Knuckles smirked. I wanted to hit him.

"Don't be stupid," I said. "Besides, we have bigger problems right now."

"Bigger problems?" Knuckles was clearly curious. "Like what?"

"Well for one thing, we're in a town called Owashia," I told him.

"Ooo, Owashia," said Knuckles pretending to be scared. "Just sneak into their computer room and send a message to Commander Lino to come get us. What's the big deal?"

"Knuckles, this isn't just an ordinary town." I was being more serious now so that he'd get the picture. "This is an underground town."

"Underground?" Knuckles freaked. "You mean we're ..."

"Yes Knuckles, Nilerm has dropped us into a secret underground world of Dysnomia," I said, "but I don't know why."

"So what are we going to do?" Knuckles asked.

"Well I'm going back to the library tomorrow," I replied, "and you are going to stay away from the princess and keep out of trouble."

"Okay, I'll stay out of trouble," Knuckles moaned. I crawled into my bed and pulled up the blankets. My stomach growled. When had I eaten last? Oh, yeah, the wedding. I yawned as it growled again. I was starving.

"Night Knuckles," I said.

"Night Layla," said Knuckles. In spite of my growling stomach, I fell instantly to sleep, waiting for tomorrow to come.

— Chapter Thirteen —

The Royal Family

I woke up and yawned. Getting out of bed, I went over to see how Knuckles and Amy were doing. Knuckles wasn't in his bed. I looked over to Amy's bed. I guess she was out of her coma because she wasn't in her bed either. Beside the door was a serving tray that had three bowls on it. Walking over to the serving tray, I discovered one bowl had oatmeal in it that looked like it had been sitting for some time while the other two bowls were empty. The oatmeal looked pretty gross to eat, but I was starving. After eating the tepid, mushy oatmeal, I walked out of the room.

I had to find out why Nilerm had put us down here and what he knew about this place. The only way I was going to find out was inside their library's history and maybe from what was in that Dark Prince book. On the second floor, I walked to the library.

"Oy!" shouted a familiar voice just as I reached it. I turned around to see Flax and Granate. "What do you think you're doing?"

"Uhh, going to the library," I said in a smart-alecky tone.

"But you have to find a job today," said Granate.

"I'll get a job tomorrow," I told them.

"Unacceptable," said Flax in a grumpy mood. Then he pointed at me. "You're getting a job today."

"Who are you, the job police?" I said, annoyed. Flax and Granate looked at each other, confused.

"What's a police?" they both asked. I rolled my eyes and walked away. But when I reached for the door, Flax and Granate grabbed me under the arms and started moving.

"Hey!" I shouted.

"Sorry Layla," Granate apologized, "but your job starts in twenty minutes."

"My job?" I was confused. "I thought you said I had to go *look* for a job?"

"Yeah, you were supposed to," Granate continued, "but the three princes of Owashia liked you so much that they hooked you up with a job."

"The Three Princes," I said. "You mean …"

"Yup," Flax interrupted. "Prince Sora, Prince Soda, and the Dark Prince. Although I don't know why they like you."

"Really, the Dark Prince, too?" We were up on the third floor now.

"Yup," Granate gulped, "even the Dark Prince."

I couldn't believe it. Prince Shaine had helped me find Amy, got a room for us, and now he had given me a job. Why was he helping me out so much?

Flax and Granate stopped walking and ushered me into a medium-sized room. There were a bunch of beanie bags on the floor and a balcony along the front wall. On the left side of the room was a stage.

"Are you Layla Jenkins?" a woman asked me. She looked like she was around Aunt Becky's age, which was early forties.

"Yes I am," I said.

"Follow me, Layla." And she walked away.

"Good Luck," said Flax and Granate as they left. I followed the lady into a changing room.

"Here." The lady held out a black and white dress for me.

"Uhh … Thank you," I said as I went into one of the changing rooms. After I put on the black and white dress, I went back into the room.

"Hold on, Layla," said the woman softly. I turned. She was holding out a rose with two colourful green leaves and a shiny, white pearl to keep it all together.

"Wow." I admired it for a moment. "It's beautiful."

"It is yours now," she said.

"Oh," I said, surprised. I took the rose and put it in my hair. "Thank you."

"You're welcome," she smiled. She bowed. "Ouvitosay."

Not sure what that word meant, I decided to repeat it. "Ouvitosay," I said as I bowed. We both stood and she walked away.

"Over here," said a quiet voice. I looked to my left. Four girls were wearing black and white dresses too, only each in her own style. With nowhere else to go, I decided to join them.

"You must be Layla Jenkins," said the same quiet voice as I went to sit down.

How did everyone know my name? "Uhh … yeah," I said, a bit creeped out now. "And you are?"

"My name is Mari," she said, "Mari Anne. I'll be working with you, along with Tan, Titi, and Tenly."

"Well it's nice to meet you all." I waved at them. But they just sat there and looked at me. "Okay then." I flicked my hair and put my hands behind me. "So what exactly are we supposed to do?"

Then they all looked at me, surprised; like no one had ever asked them that question before.

"Oh well," Mari stuttered, "we just sit here and watch."

"That's it?" I asked.

"Well, we also have to go to someone that calls us and do what they want us to do," Mari added.

"Oh … so were slaves," I said understanding now.

"What's a slave?" asked Tan confused.

They didn't know what a slave was?

"Ahh well," I tried to explained, "a slave is a person that doesn't get paid, who just sits around until their master asks them to do something. Except that we're lucky to have some freedom around here."

"Well then yeah, I guess that makes us slaves," said Tenly. I sighed.

"I hope you don't mind me asking," I said curiously, "but are you three outcasts?"

"Wow, we are." Titi was clearly amazed. "How did you know?"

"Uhh ... lucky guess," I said. Now I know why Sora thought it was weird that I knew what fraternal meant. From what I was seeing from these four, outcasts were not very smart.

"Alright, everyone." A man came in with a dorky haircut. "Get in your positions. The Royal Family is coming." The girls jumped up and ran to the places they were supposed to be.

"Royal Family?" I said.

"Yeah," Mari stuttered, "the whole family comes to see ... if it's ... the day."

"Day?" I said confused. "Day for what?"

Mari looked around to make sure no one was listening. Then she leaned in closer to me and whispered, "The day the Dark Prince finally picks his future wife."

The Dark Prince? Future Wife? I thought he was engaged to Princess Sylvia? I was going to ask Mari that question when I heard the doors opening. They were here, Prince Shaine, Prince Sora, and Prince Soda. And then I saw the three brothers' parents, the King and Queen of Owashia.

Prince Shaine definitely looked like his father. Only difference was that the King had the same bright emerald eyes as Sora. Plus, you could see that parts of his hair were going grey. The Queen was beautiful. She had long, dark, purple hair that went down to her waist. She wore her golden crown over her bangs that came down to just above her moonlight yellow eyes. She wore a silver and white dress with gold jewellery. They looked like they were in their early forties, too. The King showed it more though than the Queen. She looked as if she could be thirty-five.

"Hello your Majesty," said the dorky haired guy as he bowed down to the King and Queen. "Your Highness."

"Hello Antoine," said the King.

"Is everything ready, Antoine?" Prince Shaine asked impatiently.

"Yes, Sire." Antoine bowed down low.

"Good," said Prince Shaine. "Now let's get this over with."

"Shaine, don't be like that," said the Queen. "Love is something that you cannot rush."

"Yeah," said Soda as he put his arm over Prince Shaine shoulders. "There are so many beautiful girls here, which makes it so hard to find the right one." Soda flirted with all the girls with a wink. All the girls, except for me, flirted back at him with their sighs, giggles, or waves. I just rolled my eyes. Prince Shaine twisted Soda's arm.

"Ouch!" Soda tugged free.

"Next time you flirt with the girls," said Prince Shaine, "could you not put your arm around my shoulders?" Soda blushed in embarrassment. Sora laughed hard, while I covered my mouth and giggled.

Even though Sora's laugh hid my little laugh, Prince Shaine still must have heard me because I saw him look in my direction. I looked away quickly hoping he didn't see me. I couldn't look at him without my heart racing and my cheeks burning.

"Less talking, more walking," I heard the King say. I looked back at the Royal family.

"Right this way," said Antoine as they followed him to their seats. The King and Queen were in the front row with Prince Shaine sitting behind them, while Sora and Soda sat in the fourth row. Antoine walked up to the stage. "Ladies and gentlemen, let the show begin."

— Chapter Fourteen —

Crazy Girls

This was horrible; no wonder the Dark Prince couldn't pick his future wife. They were all the same. Each girl came onto the stage, dressed in fancy clothes, all glitter and gems. They also shared the same "special talent." And by special talent, I mean singing.

"I'll be your Queen!" squealed one of the girls. They all sucked at singing. As for their personalities, don't even get me started. All I can say are four words: bratty drama queen flirts.

"Ugh, can't anyone here sing?" I complained as I covered my ears.

"I wish I knew," said Mari. "Do you sing?"

"No, I hate singing," I lied. I loved to sing. Of course, nobody knew that. I usually sang around Aunt Becky's house when I was alone, or in the shower. I'm a pretty good singer, but I hate to sing in public.

"Thank you, Clover," said Antoine as there was an awkward applause for her. "And now our next performer is Miss Michelle,"

"Oh no," Mari whimpered.

"What? Is she the worst?" I whispered.

"Yeah, you could say that." Mari covered her ears as I did the same.

"Thank you, thank you," Michelle gloated. "I'd like to dedicate this song to my true love Prince Shaine." I rolled my eyes.

"Oh, isn't that nice Shaine," I heard the Queen say to him.

"More like creepy if you ask me," Sora whispered loudly to Soda. He laughed.

"Sora," the King scolded. Sora was quiet and Michelle began to sing.

"Oh Prince Shaine!" screamed Michelle. "Oh how I LOVVVVVVVVVVE you!"

"Ahh!" I moaned as I plugged my ears now. "This is awful. Couldn't the King and Queen hire a professional singer?"

"What's a singer?" Mari asked. I was surprised that she knew what singing was, but didn't know what a singer was. I mean the word says it all right there.

"It's what Michelle is doing," I was explaining to her, "She's singing." Then Michelle went high-pitched. "Only she's not doing a very good job."

"Well she's the best singer around here," said Mari.

Of course, why was I not surprised? From what Mari had told me about Michelle while the other girls were singing, she was the queen bee around here. Michelle was a humanoid grey fox. She was the best at everything, got all the guys, and always got what she wanted. Try to get in her way and she'd ruin your life, Mari had said. Michelle was nothing but a bully.

"Pssst, Layla?" I suddenly heard a voice whisper my name. It was Sora, calling me.

"Excuse me Mari," I said as I crept over to Sora. "You called."

"Hey Layla." Sora smiled. "How's it going?"

"You mean besides the horrible singing?" Michelle screamed and I covered my ears. "I'm alright." Then Michelle screamed even louder. "Ugh, why did you guys hire me to listen to this?"

"Don't worry, you only have to listen to this every three days," Sora whispered.

"Why?" I laughed quietly.

"So that we can help Shaine pick a bride," Sora replied. Michelle, still singing, walked down stage to cuddle with Prince Shaine.

"But I thought your brother was marrying Princess Sylvia?" I whispered, a bit angry at what I was seeing.

"He was supposed to," Sora whispered, "and he couldn't wait. But then he decided that he doesn't want to marry her anymore and wants to rule the kingdom by himself. So now, either we help him find either someone else to marry or he gets stuck with her on his twentieth birthday. Those are the rules." Michelle was leaning closer to Prince Shaine. It made my heart beat fast, but I don't know why.

"Either way, he's not too thrilled about it."

"Why Shaine's twentieth birthday?" I asked.

"Because that's when princes and princesses take the throne of their kingdom," Sora explained. "At least a part of it. We can't take full control of the kingdom until our parents are deceased."

"And you can't rule without the other half," said Soda. "There must always be a King and Queen."

"But you two are also the Princes of Owashia," I pointed out. "Don't you two want to rule the kingdom of Owashia too?"

"Oh, we already have our own kingdoms to rule," Soda said confidently.

"What do you mean you have your own kingdoms to rule?" I asked confused.

"Well ... ahh ...." Sora hesitated.

The two of them looked over to their parents and Shaine as if they were afraid that they might overhear our conversation.

"It's a long, complicated story."

After Sora spoke, we were silent for a moment. So the royalty still had arranged marriages down here. Royal arranged marriages stopped in Jurassic two-hundred years ago and in every other city on the top side of Dysnomia. Now princes and princesses could marry whomever they wanted, and if they wanted to rule their kingdom by themselves, they could. They didn't have to marry anyone in order to take over the throne.

"So what happened between them?" I asked.

"I don't know," Sora answered. "Shaine and Sylvia got into a fight one day and just like with these other girls, he doesn't want to have anything to do with her."

"If I were Shaine, I would have forgiven Sylvia four years ago," Soda told us. "I mean who cares about whatever the fight was about, she's hot."

We looked at Michelle trying to get Prince Shaine to hold her as she sang her last line. But he kept pushing her away. I smiled.

"Sometimes looks aren't everything," I told Soda.

"Except for you, babe." Soda winked at me.

"Will you knock it off already?" whispered Sora as he pushed Soda over. Everyone applauded Michelle when she stopped singing.

"Thank you, Michelle," said Antoine. "We'll take a fifteen minute break before we have the slave girls sing."

"Slaves," I said. "Oh no, I am not singing."

"But you have to." Sora smirked.

"It's the Royal Family's orders," Soda chimed in.

"Look Pri …," I said. Then Sora gave me an angry glare.

"Look Sora," I started over, "it was nice of you three to get me this job but …"

"Three?" Soda said confused.

"She's talking about you, me, and Shaine," Sora explained.

"Seriously?" Soda raised his eyebrows.

"Yup," Sora replied. He grabbed Soda and me around the neck and leaned closer. "Apparently, Layla here made quite an impression on the Dark Prince." My heart raced and I could feel my cheeks start to burn.

"Really?" I whispered as I watched Prince Shaine trying to get out of Michelle's grip now.

"Well that explains a lot," Soda whispered. "There's no way Mom and Dad would have taken on another slave girl unless Shaine suggested someone."

"Mari, you girls are up," Antoine told her.

"Right," Mari stuttered. She looked at me. "You coming Layla?"

"Actually since this is my first day," I said, "may I have permission to pass?" Antoine was not happy about that. He marched over and glared.

"Permission de …," snapped Antoine.

"Permission granted," Prince Shaine interrupted. Everyone opened their eyes wide and gasped.

"But Prince Shaine, you can't," Michelle whined. "How can we mock her if you don't let her sing?" He got out of her grip and stood back.

"For the last time, Michelle, we are not a couple," snapped Prince Shaine. "You will never be my wife and become Queen!"

"You'd think she would have figured that out four years ago," I heard one of the girls who had sung so badly say. Michelle played with her long, thick, wavy black hair, trying not to cry.

"Shaine," said the Queen as she got up, "that's no way to talk to a lady." Then Sora stood up

"Besides, Michelle's not that bad," said Sora. "I mean she could be a lot worse."

"Such as?" Shaine gave him a look.

"Well she could be this crazy girl Soda and I ran into," Sora suggested.

Crazy girl?

"Sora, Soda, you two really need to stop teasing the girls," said the King, "especially you, Soda."

"I didn't do anything." Soda looked appalled. "It was all Sora."

"And I didn't do anything either!" Sora looked just as appalled. "All I did was catch this thirteen-year-old girl when she bumped into me, and then she suddenly was talking about marriage and raising a family together."

"Yeah, it was hilarious!" Soda laughed.

Oh no, please tell me it was some other thirteen-year-old and not Amy.

"Does that ring a bell to you?" Prince Shaine smirked at me.

"No, not at all, Dark Prince," I lied.

"Please, just call me Shaine," said Prince Shaine. Everyone gasped again, including me. Our eyes widened into those deer-in-the-headlights look. I saw the King whisper into the Queen's ear just as Soda did the same thing to Sora.

All I could say was, "Okay."

We looked into each other's eyes. I was starting to feel something that I had never felt before. It was a weird but good feeling. I was also starting to see through Shaine. He might act like a mean person on the outside, but inside there was a bit of good in him. Why wouldn't he show it though? What was he hiding? Then we stopped looking at each other as Amy opened the doors and strolled in.

— Chapter Fifteen —

The Gymnasium

"Sora!" shrieked Amy as she ran towards Sora. I jumped in front of him. "Come on, Layla." Amy tried to duck around me. "You're getting in the way of destiny."

"The only destiny you have is to stay out of trouble," I told her. "Now go back to whatever you were doing before and leave Prince Sora alone."

Amy grabbed me and pushed, but she was no match for my strength. Then again, she wasn't a very strong person.

"You can't keep me away from my love!" Amy cried.

"That's enough," ordered the King as the guards came in and grabbed us.

"Hey!" Amy struggled in their grip.

"What is the meaning of this?" the Queen asked, arms crossed.

"Nothing, Mother," said Shaine. "We're just proving a point about why a woman should not be in charge."

"What?" I glared.

"You can let that slave go, boys." Shaine pointed at me. "As for the other one, take her back were she's supposed to be." That said, he walked off.

"Shaine, where are you going?" The Queen was angry now. "We're not done yet." When the guards let go of me, I ran out of the room and caught up with him.

"How dare you?" I raged.

"How dare I what?" Shaine pretended to be innocent.

"Don't play dumb with me," I said, "you know exactly what I'm talking about. How dare you insult a woman's right to lead!"

"It wasn't an insult," said Shaine. "It's just the truth."

"Excuse me!" I clenched my fists.

"If you can't control that little girl of yours," Shaine explained, "then you have no power over that stupid boy, or anyone else."

"First of all," I said, "their names are Amy and Knuckles. Secondly, just because she was goofing off doesn't mean he is."

"Oh please," said Shaine, "I bet you right now he's with MY fiancé, and at precisely 2:45 p.m. they'll come down to MY gymnasium and do some 'kissing' with each other."

"No way," I disagreed. "Knuckles may do stupid things at times, but he knows when to put his foot down and behave, especially when he gets beaten up by some little kid in front of a crowd."

"If anyone's a little kid it's you," said Shaine.

"Oh yeah?" I glared at him. "How old are you?"

"Eighteen," Shaine replied.

Darn it, he was older than me by one year.

"And you?"

I put my hands over my head. "You couldn't guess it even if you tried," I told him.

"Seventeen," Shaine grinned.

Dang it, how did he know?

"How's that for not trying?" He smirked.

I crossed my arms and frowned. "Wonderful," I mumbled.

"If you still don't believe my theory about Knuckles and Sylvia," said Shaine as he unlocked a door in the hallway, "then come inside with me and wait." I froze, shocked by his invitation.

"If you think they're together right now," I said, "then why don't we go see if you're right?"

"Because I have a schedule to stick to," replied Shaine. He

opened the door and put out his hand. "So what do you say? Are you in?" I had to think about it for a moment. Hesitating, I slowly put my hand over his.

"I'm in," I answered.

"Then come on." Shaine gripped my hand and pulled me inside. He pulled me so quickly I made a little leap in the air.

Letting go of his hand, I closed the door and the lights turned on. On the left side of the room, there were weights, exercise equipment, and gymnastic equipment. On the other side was a boxing arena with its own stage.

"Wow," I said, stunned. "This is amazing." Amazing as it was, though, it was strange. These people had technology that Jurassic had used 100-200 years ago, yet they also had things from my era that weren't invented back then, in our timeline.

"Thanks," said Shaine.

"So now what?" I asked. "We just stand here and wait?"

"Or we could do some boxing." Shaine went behind a big punching bag and held on. "You look like you box."

"Yeah, you could say that," I said and I kicked the punching bag. "Kee-yahh!"

He coughed as he fell to the floor.

"Oh I'm sorry," I said sarcastically as I grazed the punching bag and looked at him. "Did I hurt you?"

"Not bad," he replied, getting up. "For a girl."

I growled.

"Don't take me for granted your ...," Prince Shaine gave me the angry face. I sighed. "Look." I started over. "Don't take me for granted, Shaine. I'm like a wild rose—it's beautiful and innocent looking, but try to touch one and the thorns will make your fingers bleed."

"Hmm ... shall we put that to a test then?" Shaine raised his eyebrows.

"What?" I was a bit confused.

"Let's have a friendly little round and see how tough you

really are," Shaine explained. I smiled with excitement.

"Alright, I accept your challenge," I said, "but only on one condition."

"And that is?" asked Shaine.

"You are not allowed to disappear during the fight like you did to Knuckles," I told him. "And the winner proves which gender is the best."

He smiled. "Fine," Shaine agreed, "then let's begin."

— Chapter Sixteen —

Oh Knuckles ... NO!

We each stood on opposite sides of the arena. "Ready?" asked Shaine. I nodded my head. "Then let the fighting begin!"

Shaine shouted as we ran at each other. He went for a punch and I jumped over him. I flipped in the air and landed. He quickly turned around and punched again. I did a back flip and kicked him right in the chin before he could touch me.

Shaine grunted as he fell to the ground. I did a couple of cartwheels, stopped and put up my fists. He got to his feet and touched his jaw. "You like to fight hard I see."

"You think that's hard?" I grinned. "Wait 'til I'm all warmed up." When I went in to pin him down, he punched me in the stomach unexpectedly. I choked as I fell to the ground.

He pulled my arms behind my back, but I slammed my elbows into his chest and knocked him to the floor. When he let go of my arms, I turned around and pinned him to the ground stretching his arms out flat and laying my whole body on top of him.

"Surrender?" I asked. He rolled me over and pinned me in the same position.

"Never," Shaine answered. I growled with rage and managed to hit him in the shins with my knees. Shaine yelped and got off me.

While he was still on his knees, I tried to kick him in the face but he ducked. He tried to knock me down by swinging his leg under me, but I jumped just in time to avoid it. He flipped back and we were fighting head to head with each other now. When I punched his shoulder, he'd punch my shoulder. When he tried to kick me in the hip, I did the same. We were tied, with neither one of us winning. We were getting matching bruises. Shaine and I got in our last punches as we both hit each other in the cheeks. Ouch! We fell to the ground and stopped fighting to rub those last bruises.

"Shall we call it a draw?" Shaine touched his cheek again and winced.

"Yeah, good idea." I could feel my own cheek swelling.

Before I even got the chance to get myself up, Shaine was already offering his hand to help me. I grabbed his hand and he pulled me up. While he was pulling me though, I tripped and landed with my head on his chest.

"Whoops." Shaine chuckled as he caught me.

As I got myself back up, our heads touched. Our bodies were even closer as he put his arms around my shoulders. We looked into each other's eyes. My heart was pumping. I felt like I was going to explode at any moment. I let go of Shaine and walked over to the gymnastics bars.

"You know," said Shaine, "I never thought I would say this to a girl, but you're a really good fighter."

"Well I'm not your ordinary D.I.D. kind of girl," I said.

"D.I.D. girl ha," laughed Shaine. "That's a good one."

Shocked, I turned around to look at him and asked surprised, "You know what D.I.D. stands for?"

"Of course," Shaine replied. "But I'm not surprised that a smart girl like you would know it."

"Oh," I said as I sat on the elite balance beam, "and why is that?"

"Because," said Shaine as he sat on the beam with me, "it's a common phrase in fairytales—the damsel in distress."

"Oh, so you do know what it means," I teased him.

"Was there any doubt?" Shaine grabbed my hand.

I jumped a little, not expecting him to grab my hand. I felt myself blush a bit as I looked at him. He was blushing a little bit, too. Still holding on to my hand, he leaned closer to me. I don't know what he was doing, but I didn't stop him as I leaned closer to him, too. Our heads touched. We looked into each other's eyes. Then we slowly closed our eyes and moved our faces closer together—and suddenly we heard someone come in. Shaine and I looked to see who it was. Once again, Shaine was right.

Knuckles sneaked into the Dark Prince's gymnasium with Sylvia. Knuckles' hands were all over her.

"So," Knuckles flirted, reeling Sylvia closer. "Where should we start our project?"

"Oh just kiss me, you fool," Sylvia said eagerly as she squeezed herself tighter to him. With that said, they started kissing.

I was really mad that Knuckles hadn't listened to me, and Shaine looked like he was about ready to kill him.

"Knuckles!" I yelled as I jumped off the beam and walked over to them with Shaine beside me.

"Layla!" Knuckles leaped away from Sylvia. "What are you doing here?"

"Actually, the real question is what are *you* doing here with Princess Sylvia?" I glowered at him.

"And what's this 'project' of yours that you're talking about?" Shaine sounded angry.

"It's none of your business," said Princess Sylvia in a snotty tone as she let go of Knuckles.

"As your future husband you bet it's my business!" roared Shaine. "And I'm sure your father will love to hear about this little 'project' of yours too."

"Now you're dragging our parents into this," said Princess Sylvia in a whiny then angry voice. "How dare you!"

"What, because they'll think you're a big flirt, which will lead to my becoming King without having to marry a sleazy wife?" Shaine's eyes flashed. "Then I *do* dare!"

I walked over to Knuckles and grabbed him by the ear. "Come on Knuckles." I yanked him away from Princess Sylvia. "Let's leave the royal couple alone while we discuss this 'project' of yours."

— Chapter Seventeen —

Project War: Jurassic vs. Owashia

"Alright, spit it out," I growled as I let go of his ear and continued walking down the halls.

"Spit out what?" Knuckles asked, acting like he didn't know what I was talking about.

"You know exactly what I'm talking about," I said in anger. "Your 'project' with Princess Sylvia. What's this project of yours? How long have you and her been working on it? How much trouble will this get us into? Why?"

"Ugh, enough with the questions, I'll spill." Knuckles jerked his ear free in annoyance. "The project the Princess and I are working on is called project love."

"Project love," I mocked him.

"Well you see," Knuckles began, "she asked me if I loved kids and I said I love kids."

"You and kids," I laughed. "But you hate kids. When it comes to kids, you're such a big bully."

"Anyway," Knuckles continued, "Sylvia said that she loves kids too and hopes to make a family with that special someone."

My eyes widened. "Wait a minute, you're not saying," I stuttered.

"That's right," Knuckles said with pride. "Me and her are going to get married one day."

"Really," I said.

"Yup." Knuckles beamed.

"Oh," I said, and then smacked him across the back of his head.

"Ouch!" Knuckles yelped and rubbed his head.

"Are you trying to get us killed?" I yelled. "Project Love? Yuck, more like Project War!"

"I still don't get what the big deal is?" Knuckles looked confused as he rubbed the back of his head.

"The big deal?" I snapped. "The big deal is that if you break up with her like the other girls you've 'liked' and ruin her marriage to the Dark Prince, she'll send her daddy's army to destroy us. Not to mention the Dark Prince will probably send his, too."

"Others?" Knuckles looked even more confused. "What do you mean break up with her like the others?"

"Knuckles, it's your daily routine when it comes to finding 'the one,'" I explained to him. "You meet a hot girl, get all flirty with her, and then you break up with her once she falls for you."

"Well at least I'm trying to find my love!" Knuckles was really angry now. "Unlike you."

"Sticks and stones may break my bones, but your stupid words can never hurt me." I grabbed him by the ear again. "Now come on."

"Where are we going?" Knuckles yelped as he tried to pull away.

"We're going to library to find out why Nilerm has put us down here and figure out how to get the heck out of here," I explained. "It'll also keep you away from Princess Sylvia, which will keep you out of trouble with the Dark Prince."

"Hold on, you're still not off the hook about finding your own love," said Knuckles. "In fact, you're nothing but a hypocrite when it comes to love." I stopped walking and let go of his ear. I slowly tilted my head to the side and gave him a glare.

"Excuse me," I said, furious.

"Why were you with the Dark Prince in his gymnasium?" Knuckles asked curiously.

"Because he told me that at exactly 2:45 p.m. you were going to be in there with Princess Sylvia," I answered, "which he was right about, by the way."

"Oh really?" Knuckles was even more curious now. "And what did you guys do while you were waiting for us?"

"Well ... nothing really," I lied. "We just sat around arguing about who was right."

"Hah, I don't believe that one bit." Knuckles smirked. "I think you were in there with the Dark Prince just so you could kiss him."

"What?" I shrieked.

"You heard me." Knuckles smiled. As I stomped away from him, he followed. "Admit it, you don't just *like* the Dark Prince, you're in love with him."

"What?" This was *really* too much! "No, I absolutely do not like him that way. I barely even know the guy."

"Aww come on now, there's no need to be shy about it," Knuckles cooed. "Besides, this is a good thing for everyone."

"How is pretending to like Prince Shaine good for everyone?" I asked him.

"Who?" he asked confused.

"The Dark Prince," I said.

"Ahhah," said Knuckles, "That proves it right there. You knowing his name shows that you're in love with him, and ... uhh ...."

I rolled my eyes. "Stop yourself before your head explodes," I said in disgust. "But why am I not surprised? You always take things the wrong way because you're never right about anything." Then he put his hands on my shoulders. "Think about it, Layla," Knuckles began. "You pretend to like this guy and he'll ask for your hand in marriage. Not only will there never be any war between our countries, but I'll be married to one hot rich princess and you'll be married to ... a rich prince."

"Forget it," I said as I took his hands off my shoulders. We were just around the corner and heading into the library when we were interrupted by a voice.

"And where do you think you're going?" said a man in a harsh tone. Knuckles and I turned around to find Antoine, with Flax and Granate behind him.

"Uhh to the library," I said, as if it was obvious.

"Well I hate to be the bearer of bad news," said Antoine, "Actually for you two, I don't mind." He smirked. "But the library is off limits for new outcasts."

"Seriously?" I said. "For how long?"

"Until you become a proper citizen of Owashia," replied Antoine, "which should take about two or three years."

"Two or three years?" Oh, no! "Look, I don't have the time to wait that long to go to the library. If I can get permission from one of the princes ..."

"I don't care how close you are to the three princes of Owashia," Antoine interrupted, "you and your posse aren't getting into that library. Now take them away." Flax and Granate moved in to grab Knuckles and me.

"Whoa, whoa, whoa, what happened to a warning?" Knuckles leaped backward.

"You had your warning when your friend here saved your life." Flax grabbed him from behind.

"And now you get your punishment warning for ditching Sir Roger's class," said Granate.

"As for you," Antoine pointed his finger right at me. "It's time for all outcasts to go to their rooms." Antoine was walking away. "Have a good sleep."

"Okay, now you must be joking," I complained as I ran after him, with Granate following me. When I caught up with Antoine, I stopped running and followed him. "The day isn't even done yet. You don't actually expect me to sleep through the whole day do you?" Antoine stopped walking and turned to me.

"Do I have to give you the punishment warning too?" asked Antoine. "By the way, your outcast clothes are in your room." I growled under my breath. Granate grabbed my shoulder but I smacked his arm away.

"Don't touch me," I said. I walked past Antoine, storming to my room with Granate following me to make sure that I didn't try to make a run for it.

— Chapter Eighteen —

Shaine or Dark Prince?

I couldn't sleep at all. Daylight was shining on me, and I had to listen to Amy talk about how she and Prince Sora were meant for each other while I tended Knuckles' cuts and bruises. I thought the punishments here were a bit strict, but this was probably the only way Knuckles was going to learn to stay away from Princess Sylvia.

After I was finished bandaging up Knuckles, a couple of servants came in with a tray of food. There was corn, mashed potatoes, and a piece of meat they called kaboozz. It tasted like beef but with a hint of maple in it. When we were done with supper, there was nothing left to do except go to sleep since the guards had secured the area to make sure that none of us left the room.

Once it got dark, all I could hear was Amy saying *Oh Sora I love you* over and over, and Knuckles snoring. But it wasn't even their annoying sleeping habits that were keeping me awake. There were so many things that I was worried about. Like how was I going to get out of this place? How was I going to get Amy and Knuckles out of here, since they both refused to leave? And how was I going to keep them out of trouble without getting myself *in* trouble? I still didn't even know why Nilerm had put us down here. Oh my gosh, what has Nilerm been doing to Jurassic while I've been down here? I sighed.

Then I remember a song that Aunt Becky used to sing to me

when I was little. It was a song that my mom made up for me. Aunt Becky told me that my mother couldn't wait to sing it to me when I was born. Sadly though, she died when I was born so Becky tried her best to sing it to me. Apparently, my mom was a very good singer. I opened the windows and went out onto the balcony. Feeling the wind blowing on me, I closed my eyes and began to sing my mother's song.

When you're feeling down
And all alone
Don't you fear
Cause I'll be there.

When your hope is gone
And you've got nothing left to hold on to
Don't you fear
Cause I'll be there.

And when you're stuck in your life
Not sure which way to go
Just think of me
I'll be there to guide you.

It doesn't matter where you are
Or where I am
Twenty feet or two thousand miles
I will always be beside you.

So don't you cry
Keep your head up high
You don't have to be afraid
Cause I'll be there.

I smiled and listened to the silence.

"Well don't you have a lovely voice," someone spoke up. I knew that voice. I opened my eyes and leaned over the rail.

"Shaine," I said as loudly as I could without waking anyone. "What are you doing down there?"

"Same reason why you're up there," Shaine replied. I put my hand under my chin with my eyes half open.

"You couldn't sleep either," I answered. Suddenly, he jumped onto the balcony and was right beside me.

"Something like that." Shaine sat on the balcony railing. "Let's just say, she's flirting with a bodyguard named Drake right now."

"She?" I asked.

"My fiancé," Shaine replied.

"Yuck, thanks for sharing," I said disgusted, and smacked him lightly on his arm. He chuckled. Then he stopped and looked to the sky.

"So, when she does that, I come out here to practice my fighting skills," said Shaine. Then he looked at me. "What's keeping you up?"

"You mean besides my roommates?" I rolled my eyes. "Everything."

"Everything?" Shaine looked concerned.

"Hmmhmm." I nodded. It was quiet for a little while before Shaine spoke again.

"So I guess you sing that song every time you're having problems?" Shaine raised an eyebrow at me. "Man, I wish you'd told me that you could sing. I could have listened to someone who could sing well, for once."

"Thanks," I said, "my mom wrote that song for me before I was born."

"You and your mom were close?" Shaine asked.

"Sometimes I wish I knew for sure that we could have been," I said in sadness.

"What makes you say that?" Shaine asked.

"Because she died giving birth to me," I said, trying not to cry.

"Oh," said Shaine, looking a bit guilty now. "I'm sorry for your loss."

"It's okay," I said. "You didn't know."

Suddenly a beeping sound was coming from Shaine. He looked at his wrist. Wait, was that a watch he was wearing? That hadn't been there before. In fact, he was the only one I'd seen wearing a watch down here. His watch looked like our watches up top, only it was a little more advanced than ours. How could they have things that are more advanced than ours when they lived the way people in Jurassic had lived 100 to 200 years ago?

"Sylvia, what are you doing?" yelled a man. His voice was so loud that I jumped and almost slipped off the edge of the balcony.

"You have to leave now, the guards are coming." Sylvia's panicked voice came to us clearly, too.

"Right on time," said Shaine, still looking at his wrist.

"Why do you put up with her?" I asked annoyed. "You know you can marry anyone you want right?"

"Yeah." Shaine sounded a bit embarrassed.

"Then why?" I asked, a little calmer now.

"I don't know." Shaine shrugged. "She's better than the other girls that my parents pick for me. I can't stand any of them. I just want to be King and rule alone."

"But you have to marry or else …?" I prompted.

"Or else I can't become King."

"I'm not sure if this has ever occurred to you," I suggested, "but why don't you pick the type of girl you would like to have as your Queen or at least tell your parents what kind of girls you like?"

Shaine shrugged. "Because I don't have a type I like."

"Sure you do," I said. "Everyone has a type they like."

"Well I haven't met my type yet," said Shaine. "What about you?"

"Me?" I looked away. "Well … no, not yet."

"That's what I thought." Shaine's expression was hard to read.

"Well then why don't you pick a girl that has what it takes to be your Queen? You know, someone that makes you look good as King?"

"Hmm," said Shaine. "Well I don't want to marry a fool, that's for sure." I giggled at what he said. He hmmed again and got up. "But it's too late now. I've had four years to at least find someone else to marry before I become heir to the throne. Today was my last chance my parents have informed me. Sylvia and I get married in six weeks and there's nothing I can do. I'm stuck with her forever now."

His words stung me. He was getting married to Princess Sylvia in six weeks. Why did it hurt me so much? It felt as if someone had stuck a knife through my heart. Like the blood unexpectedly had stopped flowing through my veins. Why was this even bothering me? Their wedding had already been arranged long before I came along, and I still barely knew the guy. He was so confusing, too. One minute he was all I-will-destroy-you and then the next he was all caring and helping. Well, I didn't care what he did. It wasn't my problem.

"Oh by the way," said Shaine as he got off the balcony railing, "you don't have to worry about singing while you're working. I told my assistant Antoine …"

"Antoine?" I bolted to me feet. "Antoine works for you?"

"Yes." Shaine tilted his head, surprised. "Is that a problem?"

"No, not at all," I lied. Those weren't the words I wanted to say. I should have asked Shaine for permission to go into the library, but I didn't want to get into trouble.

"Anyway," Shaine continued, "I told him to make sure that you don't sing until I come back. Which I'm glad I did."

"Back?" I said, worried, as I hopped off the railing of the balcony too. "Where are you going?"

"I'll be out exploring for three weeks," Shaine answered. "My last days of freedom."

"Going to use your last days of freedom to find your dream girl?" I joked. "It's never too late."

"Hmm," said Shaine. "Tell you what, when you figure out what type of guy you like, then I'll tell you what my dream girl is like. I should have it figured out by then. Deal?"

"Deal," I agreed as we shook hands.

There was that feeling again. He let go of my hand and was leaving. As he left, though, he turned back to face me and turned his frown into a smile. He winked at me. "See you in three weeks."

Before I could ask any more questions, he jumped on to a couple of more balconies and was gone. I leaned my shoulder against the wall and smiled. I don't care, huh? So then, why did I want to get to know the "real" Dark Prince even more?

— Chapter Nineteen —

They're Gone!

Time sure seemed to fly by around here. After almost three weeks, it still felt as if Prince Shaine had left only yesterday. Work was going well and easy. Sure the girls' singing was still horrible, but I manage to tune them out now.

Since I didn't have to sing with the other slave girls, I mainly talked to Sora and his fiancé Sal. Actually, Sal was supposed to be Sora's wife by now, but because Shaine and Princess Sylvia were having problems, their parents had to postpone the prince's wedding until Shaine and Princess Sylvia worked it out or he found somebody else to marry. I didn't understand why all three of them had to marry at the same time.

The last time I talked to Soda was before he left to see his fiancé, Flora. He told me that it was important to their parents that the three of them marry at the same time because they wanted to make sure that when they were gone, their sons would all be okay. They wanted to help their sons find a soulmate and make them happy as much as possible while they were still around.

However, Sora and Soda couldn't wait anymore. They just wanted to be with their loved ones and move forward. Their parents, however, didn't appreciate it. Amy was really upset when she found out that Sora already had his own fiancé, but at least she would stay away from him and keep herself out of trouble.

I could see why Sora loved Sal so much. She was definitely his kind of girl. She was beautiful both inside and out, with long, thick, chocolate brown hair and sky blue eyes, and a couple of visible freckles on her face. Sal had the body of a model, tall and skinny. She was a really shy person, but once she got to know you it would go away. She was girly, but she did have a bit of tomboy in her.

This was ridiculous. It was bad enough for their parents to make them wait to get married because Shaine didn't have a fiancé yet, but why would the King and Queen keep their sons away from their fiancés? Mari Anne told me once that Sora and Soda had to stay away from them for their own sakes. Apparently, the King and Queen were afraid that Shaine would be jealous of his brothers' happiness and kill their fiancés. At least that was the rumour.

Now that Shaine wasn't around, I was starting to hear a lot of rumours about him and how he became the Dark Prince. Some said that he killed Princess Sylvia's first boyfriend and was forcing her to marry him. Others said that one person didn't agree with one of his rules, so he cut that person into pieces and said that if anyone else disagreed with him they would share the same fate. But what made Shaine the Dark Prince was his favourite hobby. Every night, he would hide in the shadows and wait for someone that he could slay. He liked to take life away from anyone or anything the minute he got the chance. He was a killer, or so the whispers rumours went.

Everyone else might be sucked in by these rumours, but I wasn't. I never believe in rumours. Besides Knuckles, Shaine had shown no violent behavior to anyone since I'd been here. Even if he had told me that he would kill Knuckles and me if I didn't keep my word, he still gave me a chance to live. If he was a Dark Prince, he would have killed us right there instead of letting us live. Maybe he was a little cold and distanced from everyone, but maybe he was the kind of guy that liked being alone and wasn't afraid to speak his honest opinion. So every time a group of people gathered together and began to speak of the Dark Prince, I'd always walk away and say I didn't want to hear it. If Shaine was really a murderer, I would find out from him.

During the time he was gone, I finally understood why Shaine couldn't stand any of the girls his parents had picked for him. They were fakes. When Mari and I had to work for them, all they talked about was how each of them were going to trick Shaine into falling in love with them and what they were going to do with his money. It sickened me. They didn't want to marry him for who he was. They just wanted the money. Worst of all, his parents didn't notice or even care that they were a bunch of fakes. It really ticked me off. And while Shaine was gone, those little gold diggers had of course been flirting with other guys. Nothing new there. Urr, why was I getting overwhelmed over this?

Knuckles had been chasing Princess Sylvia at the beginning, but after a few days, he stopped. In fact, he hadn't gotten into trouble for a while now. I didn't know what changed his mind, but at least I didn't have to worry about him. For now.

As for me, when I wasn't working, and when Antoine didn't have his eyes on me, I would sneak into the library every chance I could, to get more information about this place and how to get home. This underground world didn't make any sense.

The way they got things to work, the way they acted, how they had things from the past alongside things from today. While we got electricity from generators, wires, motors, batteries, whatever we could use to get the negative and positive electrons continuously flowing together in a path to make an electrical circuit, they got their electricity down here from a stone called an electra stone. They put this stone under the castle in a plastic box connected to a bunch of wires and voila, everything that used electricity worked, from turning on the lights to turning on those two computers.

They also had this special kind of white powder with blue specs in it they used to clean the castle. They would just throw this stuff on anything that was dirty and use a mop, sweeper, dry towel to move it around, and whatever you were cleaning was instantly clean. And I mean anything. Carpet, wood, stone, cement, you name it. This powder kept the castle so clean that you didn't really need to wear shoes around here. I wish I'd had this powder when I accidently stained my Aunt Becky's rug when I was eight.

And the technology here is what made this place the strangest. They had the two computers, watches, carriages that used robotic horses instead of regular horses, and their medical care was up to Jurassic standards. Heck, they might even be further than we were with medical care, especially when they used those green bandages on my hand when it was broken and it healed immediately. But they had no vacuums, no cellphones, no TVs. They didn't even know what police were, and yet they had all of these other things. This just didn't make any sense. It just seemed to go against science.

As for finding a way back home, I was getting nowhere. There was nothing I could find in the books that gave me any information about how to get back up to the top side. But I wasn't going to give up. I knew there was a way to get back home and whatever it was, I would find it.

But today I wasn't working and the library was off limits, so I decided to go back to my room and take it easy. There was something weird about this day, though. It was quiet, everyone was happy, and I had time to myself to relax. It was all just … too normal. I would have figured by now that Amy or Knuckles were up to something, but there was no evidence to prove it. I guess it was just one of those lazy days. So I went into my bedroom and lay down on my bed. Eyes closed, I cleared my mind of all thoughts and relaxed.

"Oy, hurry up will you!" shouted a familiar voice. I opened my eyes and quickly ran onto the balcony. It was Flax, along with Antoine and Granate.

"I'm going as fast as I can." Granate was carrying a box of weapons. Flax was also carrying a box of weapons and Antoine was freaking out. What was going on? I bent down and peeked over the edge so that they couldn't see me.

"Oh … this is not good, this is not good," said Antoine wringing his hands. "How could I let this happen? When Prince Shaine finds out, he's going to kill me."

"Calm down, Antoine," said Flax. "You know the Dark Prince is not going to kill you."

"Besides, we'll bring the princess back before he comes home tomorrow," said Granate in confidence. Princess Sylvia! Bring her back? Where did she go? Oh no, tell me he didn't ....

"So what do you want us to do with Knuckles?" asked Flax. Knuckles!

"If you see him, kill him," Antoine snarled. "And if you run into his friends, get rid of them, too."

"Yes sir," said Flax and Granate.

No, this couldn't be true. Knuckles couldn't be behind this. There was no proof.

Was there?

I went back into the room and looked around. Under the beds, behind the curtains, and finally I looked inside the drawer. There I found a container and a note. I grabbed the container first to see what it was. Sleeping pills! The container read: *Just put the pill in cold water and you'll be out like a light!*

That dirty, rotten, little jerk. He hadn't been leaving Princess Sylvia alone. He had been sneaking off at night to see her. And to make sure that I didn't get suspicious and start to follow him, he had slipped sleeping pills in my water. I threw them back in the drawer and read the note.

Hey Layla, I read and I could hear his voice already, *Sorry about the sleeping pills I've been putting in your water, but you along with the rest of world were keeping me away from Princess Sylvia. I know right now you're thinking that I just love her because she's hot and I'm making a big mistake that's going to get us killed, but you're wrong. I do love Sylvia. She different from the other girls I've met before. I'm going to marry her and then we'll start our life together. Just go home okay? Everything is going to be fine. Your friend, Knuckles. P.S. I brought Amy with me to Besha so you don't have to worry about her.*

He's a dead man. I ran out of the room to get some help from Sora, but someone was calling me.

I turned around to see that it was Mari Anne.

"Hey Mari," I said. "Look, I don't want to be rude, but I don't have time to chit chat with you today, okay?"

"But it's about Prince Sora," said Mari.

"Sora," I said. "What's wrong with Sora?"

"It's horrible Layla," Mari cried. "Last night, Prince Sora went to go get something when some guy beat him up. I guess he was kidnapping Princess Sylvia."

"What!" I said, horrified. Knuckles! The news kept getting worse. "Oh my gosh, is he alright?"

"He's fine," said Mari. "Dr. Beak said it was just a few broken ribs, but from the look of his bruises, I thought he was going to die. Speaking of Prince Sora, he wanted to see you right away, Layla."

"Right, I'll go talk to him now," I said as I ran past her. "Bye, Mari."

How could he do this? Beating Prince Sora up was probably going to cost us a war between our countries. And running away with the Dark Prince's fiancé was going to get us all killed. Err, why couldn't he just listen to me for once?

Inside the waiting room, I saw Dr. Beak talking to one of the nurses. He saw me and walked up to me.

"Layla," said Dr. Beak, "Sora has been waiting for you. Follow me please."

In his room, Sora was sleeping on the hospital bed. Knuckles had really beaten him. Bandages wrapped his body, chest, and his head. He had bruises almost everywhere and a bleeding cut that went from his forehead to his lips. He had IVs in both arms.

"Your majesty," said Dr. Beak gently, "Layla is here as you requested." He slowly opened one eye. Then he closed it. "Thank you Dr. Beak," said Sora. "That'll be all."

"Right," said Dr. Beak. "Press the button if you need me." The doctor left the room.

"Sora, I'm ..." I tried to apologize.

"Just listen, Layla," interrupted Sora. "You have to stop Knuckles before he starts a war against Jurassic."

"Jurassic," I said surprised. "How do you ...?"

"You were too smart to be an outcast," Sora interrupted. "So I snuck into Shaine's computer room and checked out your ID profile. I saw that you live in Jurassic, which is on the top side of Dysnomia. I made a new ID profile about you and put it into the other computer in the information room."

"Oh." I hesitated.

"Don't worry, this is our little secret." Sora winked at me. With my hand over my heart, I sighed with relief.

"Thank you," I said.

Sora slowly nodded his head a little.

"There's something I still don't understand though," I said. "I thought you guys couldn't get information about Overlanders on your computer. So how is your brother getting all this information about Overlanders?"

"I'm not entirely sure myself," said Sora. "He made that computer in his room by himself so his computer is definitely more advanced than our own computer, but not enough to get information about Overlanders. The only thing I can think of is maybe he found a piece of something from the topside world and scanned it on his Iden to get the information on his computer."

"The what?" I asked confused.

"The Iden," said Sora. "It's a device Shaine made that helps get us information on our enemies or anything in particular. You just take a piece of something from a particular area and voila, you have all the information on that place. Pretty neat, huh?"

"It's possible," I agreed. "But even if that's true, where would he have gotten an overland item? My friends and I ditched all of our overland stuff when we got captured."

"Hmm," Sora pondered. "Maybe this will help you out." He nodded toward a bag beside the bed. "Look in my bag." I did.

"The Dark Prince's book," I said, amazed.

"Well it's actually his journal," said Sora, "but I think it'll help you answer some of your questions." Suddenly, we heard the sound of horses whinnying. "You don't have that much time, Layla. You have to hurry and hitch a ride with Flax and Granate."

"Right," I said as I ran off. Outside, where the pool was, I ran to the left tower where it leads to the carriages.

"Come on men," said a voice. I quickly hid behind the bushes. A couple of bodyguards came out and ran into the castle. I ran down the tower stairs. At the bottom, I peeked around the corner to see where Flax and Granate's carriage was. When I found it, I saw that they were still loading weapons in it. How much did they need?

"Are we almost done?" I heard Granate complain.

"Yeah, just a few more boxes of ammo," answered Flax as they walked away. "Now come on." Inside the carriage were spears, swords, axes, bows and arrows, huge hammers, knives, and some guns. I quietly ran over to the carriage and checked out a green box. It held bows and once I took them out and hid them in some nearby bushes, I could fit into it with no problems.

"Gone!" I heard Antoine shout. I gasped and quickly climbed inside the green box. Yep, tight fit, but I could close the lid. "What do you mean they're gone?"

"They're gone," replied Flax.

"Yeah, nobody's seen that Amy girl since yesterday," added Granate.

"And as for Layla," said Flax.

"She's probably out there right now looking for them," said Granate.

"Well, good luck on your mission," said Antoine. "And remember; bring back the princess safe and sound. We don't want Prince Shaine to find out about any of this."

"Yes, sir," said Flax and Granate in unison. With that said, the carriage started moving and I was on my way to a new adventure.

— Chapter Twenty —

The Deal

I figured we were on the road for at least five hours. Wherever Flax and Granate were going, it must be very far away from Owashia. Quietly, I opened the lid a crack to let in some light, grabbed the Dark Prince's journal, and read the first content page.

"Let's see," I whispered. The day Prince Shaine was born, his childhood, battles, marriages to Gemstone, Salma, Jurassic ... JURASSIC!

I flipped to page 101 and continued reading.

Saturday, July 24. Once again, I have run into another Overlander. He was a short and fat man with greyish-white hair, dark brown eyes, and a long crooked nose. He said his name was Nilerm.

Nilerm! So he had been down here. Question is what did he do to get out of here alive?

When I brought him back home as a prisoner, he begged me to let him live and said he would give me anything I wanted. But there was nothing that pathetic, greedy, little Overlander could give me.

That was until he mentioned the princess of his country. Rose I think her name was—Princess Rose of Jurassic. Anyway, Nilerm told me that if I let him go, I could marry Princess Rose and rule half of the overworld.

It was tempting, but a risky deal. If I took it, there could be a good chance that I was being tricked and our underground world would be exposed to those Overlanders. But if I didn't take it, then I would also lose the chance of taking over the world above. Tempting as it was though, it was not worth the risk for my home.

So I rejected his deal and decided to leave him in the desert. He had nowhere to go. There was only one way he could ever get back up to his own world and it is completely impossible. Let one of the Outcast tribe take him in and good riddance.

That little traitor. Nilerm almost put Jurassic into great danger with these people just so he could save his own butt. Now I really had to find Knuckles and stop him from doing something stupid. Especially since I now knew there was a way to get back home. I didn't know how I was going to find this place Shaine was talking about, but I'd find a way to get him to tell me. As I started to close the lid, someone yanked it wide open and grabbed me.

"Oy, what do we have here," I heard Granate say as he pulled me out of the box.

I screamed. Flax stopped the carriage, Granate jumped out and pinned me to ground. Flax got out of the carriage and stood over Granate.

"Looks like we've got ourselves a stowaway," said Flax.

"Hey guys," I said, "what's up?"

"Nothing much," replied Flax, "Antoine just gave us orders to kill you and your crew."

"So I've heard," I said. "Don't do this, guys. If we work together, we can find Knuckles and Princess Sylvia before something bad happens."

"How do you know all this?" Granate looked astonished.

"Because she's been watching us." Flax grabbed a spear. "And I don't like being spied on."

"Hold on," I said. "If you kill me, the princes won't be happy about this." Granate loosened his grip on me.

"She's got a point you know," he agreed.

"What?" Flax shouted. "Have you lost it?"

"Come on now Flax, just think about it," said Granate. "Soda always buys a new slave girl so he can flirt with her, and we know Sora likes to help someone in need. But the Dark Prince ... Layla's the only girl he's ever asked his parents to buy."

"Look, I'm not the bad guy here," said Flax. "I don't want to kill Layla either. I don't think she deserves to be killed, but it's Antoine's orders and she *has* broken her promise to the Dark Prince."

Right, my promise.

"There's nothing we can do."

He spoke the truth. I could see by the way his hand holding the spear shook; he really didn't want to do this. As he was ready to strike, a blunt-tipped arrow hit his hand and he dropped the spear.

"Ouch!" Flax shook his bruised hand.

"What the ..." Granate stood up and let go of me. Then a couple more arrows with nets attached to them arced towards Flax and Granate.

They both screamed as the net entangled them.

Suddenly a bunch of men and teenage boys, wearing the same clothes as I was, came roaring towards us. One of the boys helped me up.

"Are you alright?" he asked.

"Yes," I answered uncomfortably.

"Good," said an older man who appeared from behind me.

"Oy, outcasts," said Flax in anger. "Let us go right now or else .... "

"You shall be quiet!" shouted the boy who had helped me up and he pointed a spear at Flax's face. "How dare you try to take more of our women?"

"What?" Granate looked shocked.

"Let's take them away," said the boy and the outcast men dragged Flax and Granate away. The boy came back to me.

"Thanks for saving me," I said gratefully as I followed them to where their tribe had camped.

"You married?" he asked eagerly.

"Excuse me?" I gave him a sideways look.

"You married?" he said more seriously now, as other outcast men came over. It was weird to hear a boy who was two years younger than me ask if I was married.

"Do I have a ring on my finger?" I asked sarcastically. It was quiet for a minute and then they all laughed.

"That's a good one," a man called out.

"Yeah, what's a ring got to do with anything?" Another man chuckled.

"What's a ring?" another asked and they laughed even harder now.

Well I guess that explained why they found it funny.

"I'm only seventeen," I said sharply.

"Seventeen huh?" The boy smirked. "I've never been married to an older woman before."

"Well that's not gonna happen," I told him.

"She's right," said one of the older men. "She should be with someone older." Then he grinned. "Like me."

I object!

"That's not fair," said a younger man in anger. "You already have three wives."

Three wives!

"If you want to win her, you have to go through me," he replied.

When did I turn into a prize to be won? The boy that helped me up punched him in the face and they all began to fight. Staying out of it, as if I could, I jogged over to the other outcast men that were dragging Flax and Granate along.

"So how far away are we from … home?" I asked one of them.

"Not far," said the outcast that was beside me.

He was right. We walked in the flat desert for only about fifteen or twenty minutes before we reached a bright, vibrant green tropical area, their territory.

— Chapter Twenty-One —

Meeting Mama Dara

I couldn't believe what I was seeing. We went suddenly from a sandy desert to a tropical rainforest. There we came to their home base. It was amazing. A huge, ancient temple made of stone was covered with vines. Down in the center of the whole place was a space of trampled dirt and some broken ruins from the temple. There was also some kind of weird stool in the middle of the dirt space, too.

"Take those two to the meeting gathering," ordered the older man, the one with three wives. The four outcast men holding on to Flax and Granate did as he said and went down some stairs.

"Everyone else run to the people and tell them that the chief has called a meeting." All the outcast men ran in different directions to tell their people the news while I decided to explore until the meeting started. They'd just got back so it was probably going to take awhile.

This place was amazing. As I walked through the halls, the sunlight shone on me from broken gaps in the temple's roof. Huge pillars at each end held up the roof, rather than solid walls, so you had a clear view of the jungle. Outside the temple walls were huts and tents in the grass and dirt where the people lived. I stepped onto soft ground.

"Eww gross," I said in disgust. I lifted my dirty foot and wiped off the muck. My feet were really rough and dry. I hadn't worn shoes for such a long time that I didn't even notice. I think the last time I wore shoes was when I was at the wedding and announced as the next Royal Commander. "Looks like it's going to take awhile to get my feet back to normal if this keeps up."

"Do you need shoes?" I heard a little girl ask. I looked up to see a girl that was probably two years older than my cousin Nikki. She was half-humanoid with short, brown hair, cat ears, and a tail.

"Actually I do," I said. "Do you know where I could get some?"

"Follow me," said the little girl. We went around the corner, at the end of another hall took a right turn, and outside the temple there was a small hut. "Mama Dara, Mama Dara!" She ran into the hut and I walked over to it.

"Hello," I said as I peeked through the door.

"Come on in, child, come in." Mama Dara stepped out of the shadows. "There's nothing to be afraid of."

I did as she said and went inside. She was half-humanoid too, with white and grey coloured hair, yellow eyes, and a few age spots on her face. She had owl ears and bits of feathers were hiding under her dark brown dress and cloak. From the looks of her wrinkles, I guessed that she was around her early seventies. "Can I help you with something?" she asked me.

"Uhh, yes," I answered. Then I looked at the girl. "This little cutie here brought me over to get some shoes." They both looked at my feet.

"Ahh, I see," said Mama Dara. "Darcy, will you please go get me the 'special' sandals while I work on her feet?"

"Okay." Darcy smiled and disappeared into the back.

"Oh no, that won't be necessary," I told Mama Dara. "I'd just like some shoes to wear."

"But I insist," said Mama Dara. "Now would you kindly sit for me?"

"Uhh, okay," I said as I sat on a chair. She grabbed both my feet and put some weird, slimy, green stuff on them.

"There," said Mama Dara as she rubbed my feet.

The green goo glowed and then started to disappear. When she was done rubbing my feet, I grabbed them both and was amazed at how smooth they were again.

"Wow," I said stunned, "that's amazing. What's in that stuff?"

"It's my special potion for healing feet." She smiled widely. "For only Mama Dara to know."

"I've got the sandals, Mama Dara," Darcy said cheerfully as she returned and handed a pair of sandals to her.

"Thank you Darcy," said Mama Dara as she took them. "Here you go, darling."

These sandals were stunning. They were a light brown colour like hot chocolate, with beads on a string, and a seashell shaped like a heart to hold it all together.

"Wow, these are beautiful," I said. "How much are they going to cost?"

"Oh no, this is a gift from me to you," said Mama Dara.

"A gift?" I was a bit confused.

"Yes, a thank you gift for everything you will be giving Darcy and every other outcast girl, a better future," said Mama Dara. "Your wedding day will bring everyone happiness."

"Excuse me?" I said, making sure I had heard her correctly.

"Your name is Layla, isn't it?" asked Mama Dara.

"Yes," I answered.

"Besides being the oldest and widest lady around, I am also the psychic of this place," Mama Dara explained, "and in your future, I see that you find love. Each step you take on your journey will lead you soon to marriage and happiness."

Love ... in my future?

"I'm sorry, you must be talking about another Layla," I told her, "Because my journey is to find my friends and get us back home. And once we're home, I'll be joining the top Royal Commanders."

"Ahh, I see." Mama Dara looked at the sandals I was wearing, then smiled and looked back at me. "Tell me, do you always follow your heart?"

"Of course," I said with confidence, "my heart has never let me down." She sighed.

"Then I guess your destiny is certain," said Mama Dara. Bells began to ring.

"What's going on?" I asked.

"The execution is about to start," said Mama Dara.

"Execution," I mumbled. Oh no, Flax and Granate.

"Darcy and I don't usually go to these things. We're killing people that are our only hope for a better future," explained Mama Dara. "Like you and your friends, some of us get taken to their castles by force and we get educated. As an Overlander, you can see that we outcasts aren't exactly the smartest bunch." The bell rang louder. "You'd better hurry and go."

"Right," I said as I ran out of the room. Then I stopped at the door. "Uhh … about me being an Overlander."

"Don't worry child," said Mama Dara, "Your secret is safe with me. Consider this another gift."

"Thanks," I said. Then I ran off to the meeting gathering.

I understood why Mama Dara thought it was such a waste that they were killing people that were only trying to help make their lives better. I saw two men fighting over a girl, and boys threw rocks at each other while the girls played with their dolls.

— Chapter Twenty-Two —

Chief Tinu and His Children

At the meeting gathering, the people screamed *Chief! Chief! Chief!* Flax and Granate had been put into stocks in the far left corner with guards in front of them. I quietly ran over to them.

"So ...," I said, "how's it going?"

"Ha-ha, you're hilarious," said Flax sarcastically. "Now get us out of here."

"I don't even know if I even want to," I told him, "or should for that matter."

"We promise we won't kill you," Granate said earnestly. "We'll all just pretend that Antoine didn't give us any orders. Nobody really likes him anyway."

"Forget it," I said. "If you want out, it's gonna cost you."

"What do you want?" Flax sounded annoyed.

"Take me to wherever Knuckles is and promise you won't kill him, Amy, or me."

"No deal." Flax scowled.

"Deal," Granate said quickly.

"Granate," Flax whined.

"What? She's our only way out of here."

"Err ... fine." Flax made a face. "You've got yourself a deal. So make it snappy."

"Quiet everyone, quiet," yelled an outcast man in the center of the meeting gathering. Beside him was a man I assumed was the Chief. Everyone did as he said and bowed down. I went on my knees and pretended to bow.

The Chief was a very big man wearing a long, feathered chief hat that glowed green. He wore a brown, leather shirt and pants with white and yellow strips at the edges. He had tattoos on his cheeks of a polka dotted star inside a triangle.

"My people," yelled the Chief, "we are here today to go over our biggest rule. Long ago, strange people came to our homes and took our people away to their lands. To stop them from taking more of us, we started a war. But both sides were losing lots of people."

"Anytime you want to get us out would be great," said Flax in annoyance.

"I'm working on it," I whispered.

"So we made a deal with these strange people," the Chief continued. Then four outcast men dragged someone forward. His face was hidden by a bag over his head and his hands were tied. "The deal was that we would allow them to take some of our people to their home. But they were only allowed to take away a few of us, and within fifty miles of our own homes."

One of the outcast men took the bag off the prisoner's face, cut the ropes that tied his hands, and held him by the hair. I gasped when I saw who it was.

"Shaine," I mumbled.

"But today the Dark Prince has broken that deal by trying to take another outcast woman away from our home," the Chief yelled.

"For the last time Tinu, I wasn't trying to steal any of your people," Shaine shouted.

"Oh no," said Chief Tinu. "If you were not trying to whatever this 'steal' word means, then why are these two here?"

He pointed at Flax and Granate. All they could do was smile innocently.

"Hello your majesty," said Flax nervously. Shaine clenched his hands.

"Flax, Granate!" roared Shaine. "You two better have a good reason why you're out here."

"Uhh ... well ... you see," said Flax stumbling to find his words.

"It's ... uhh ... it's like this," stuttered Granate.

"Enough!" screamed Chief Tinu. "What is done is done."

He didn't see me. "Hey guys," I whispered, "how come I didn't get in trouble with Chief Tinu for being over here?"

"Because you're an outcast woman," replied Flax.

"Lovely," I said sarcastically.

"The question now is what will be their punishment?" Chief Tinu asked.

"Death! Death! Death!" the crowd screamed.

"Death to the Dark Prince it is then," ordered Chief Tinu. "Put him on the execution table." I gasped.

"Quick, give me some information on Chief Tinu," I whispered.

"You don't know anything about your own Chief in your own homeland?" Flax sounded shocked.

"I never said I was born here," I told him.

"Then which outcast tribe are you from?" asked Flax.

Curse Flax and his questions.

"Does that really matter right now?" Granate snapped quietly. "Just give the girl what she wants."

Shaine was struggling to break the four outcast mens' grip and get off the table.

"Okay, okay, uhh ...," Flax looked thoughtful. "He holds the record of being married to twenty wives, he likes to hunt, and his favourite animal is the cookie."

"The food," I said annoyed.

"No, the actual animal, the cookie," said Flax.

What was wrong with this place? "That's no good," I whispered. "What about kids, he has to have some kids with twenty wives?"

"Yeah, he's got two sons and lots of daughters," said Flax.

Then an outcast man who looked like he was in his early twenties appeared with an axe in his hand. He had long, black hair that was all beaded. Some of his beads were in the shape of tiny skulls. He had glowing green eyes and the same markings on his face as the Chief. He wore no shirt, like most of the young men that I'd seen around here, and you could see a tattooed skull on his left arm. He wore ragged brown pants that went to his knees.

"The one who is going to kill Shaine is his oldest son, Clint. And the younger is the red, freckle faced boy named Shamu, who's over there." I looked and saw that the ten year old boy was alone and defenceless.

"I know how we're going to get out of here," I said. "Be right back."

"Wait, where are you going?" was the last thing I heard Granate say.

Quietly, I crawled up to one of the guards and took his knife as he watched the scene at the table. Finding a sharp rock that looked like a knife, I tucked the knife away at my left side and took the rock. I quickly sneaked up on Shamu, as close as I could get so that I could make a surprise attack. Desperate times call for desperate measures. Clint leaned over Shaine.

"Any last words, Dark Prince?" Clint asked. I ran for Shamu and grabbed him.

"I do," I said as I held him and put the stone to his throat. "Let go of Prince Shaine right now or else the boy gets it." Everyone looked as if they weren't sure if I was serious. Especially Chief Tinu. Clint however, seemed to be amused by this.

"If you don't believe me, check your weapons," I told the Chief. The Chief nodded and the guards all checked their weapons.

"She took my knife," growled one of the guards. Tinu looked back at me in anger.

"Little girl, you better let go of Prince Shamu before I decide to kill you with the Dark Prince," ordered Chief Tinu.

"I can kill your son before any of your guards lay a finger on me," I told him. "Look, it's not a hard choice to make. Just let go of Prince Shaine and I let go of Prince Shamu." Chief Tinu was clearly thinking about it.

"Do as my lady says," Clint ordered.

My lady? Oh no, he did not just call me *his* lady.

"Let him go," Tinu growled. Stunned, the four outcast men slowly let go of Shaine. He looked at me in total surprise.

"Uhh, Layla," Flax coughed. I moved over to the stocks.

"Let them go too," I demanded. The two guards looked at Clint.

"You heard her," said Clint. "Let them go." They did as he said and let Flax and Granate go. Once they were out of the stocks, they made a bolt for it.

"Thanks Layla," Granate called over his shoulder.

"We'll come back and save you," said Flax. Shaine followed them and I slowly walked backwards in the direction they had run off.

"Clint my son, what have you done?" Chief Tinu asked in anger.

"She is the most beautiful girl I've ever seen father," said Clint, "and she must be mine."

"You do realize I'm threatening your brother's life here?" I told him.

"All the more attractive to me," said Clint. What a sick man. He took a few steps towards me, but I took a few steps back. "There is no need to be scared. Marry me and become my Queen. With you by my side, we will rule the whole world." I shook my head slowly, frightened by his twisted ideas.

"Sorry, Clint, but I don't think she's interested," said Shaine.

Bless him, he hadn't run off with Flax and Granate. I felt his presence at my shoulder.

Clint smirked. "Well it's a good thing her parents taught her that she can't say no when a man asks her to be his wife," said Clint. "That's even a bigger no when it comes to royalty."

"Well until the day you become a man, she's safe," said Shaine. Clint's smirk turned to a frown. "We're out of here."

I let go of Prince Shamu and turned to make a run it, but Shaine was one step ahead of me. He swept me into his arms and ran.

"It wasn't a knife, it was a rock," shouted another guard.

"Shoot him!" screamed Clint. I felt the wind of arrows zipping past us and held on to Shaine more tightly. I couldn't believe how fast he was going. He was going so fast that I didn't even notice when he finally stopped running.

"You can let go of me now," said Shaine. I opened my eyes and saw that we were back in the dry desert. He gently put me down and I let go of him.

"I've never met anyone that fast before," I said amazed. "What was that, sonic speed?"

"Something like that." Shaine smiled,

"Is that how you disappeared during the fight with Knuckles?" I asked.

"Hmm … that's a good thought," said Shaine, "But no. If I was using my speed to disappear, you would have felt the rush of wind pass by you."

"Right, well …" I said. Shaine walked a couple of paces ahead of me. "Huh, there's a tiny arrow in your butt."

"What!" Shaine freaked. He looked at his behind and saw the tiny arrow stuck in his butt. "Oh that's just great. Looks like I'll be stuck like this for the rest of my life."

"Calm down, there's no need to panic," I said calmly. "I can get that little arrow out."

"What?" Shaine leaped away from me. "Oh no, forget it. You're not pulling anything out of me."

"Don't be such a baby," I said. "It will only take a couple of seconds."

"Yeah right." Shaine kept his distance. "That's like saying I'll hand over my kingdom to you. There has to be another way."

"Will you just …," I said. He zigged, I zagged, and we slammed into each other and went down. Hard.

"Whoa!" Shaine held on to my head and body as we hit the ground. On the ground, Shaine got onto his hands and knees. "You okay?" he asked still leaning above me.

"I'm fine." I smiled. He smiled back.

"Ahem," said a voice. We looked over to see Flax and Granate standing a few paces away from us.

"Well this explains a lot," said Granate.

"Nooo, it's not what it looks like." Shaine got up quickly.

"Really? Your blushes aren't helping your case," said Flax.

"Seriously, there's nothing going on between us," said Shaine. While he wasn't paying attention, I waited for the right time to pull the arrow out. "As you can see." He showed them the arrow. "Chief Tinu's warriors shot me. So Layla here was just …," I yanked the arrow out. He yelled and all three of them looked at me like scared little boys as I tilted the arrow up and down. "Ouch."

"Are you alright, your majesty?" asked Granate.

"I'm fine," Shaine whispered painfully. "Never better."

"Glad to hear it," I said. "Now take off your pants."

"What!" they all said. I rolled my eyes at their reaction.

"If you don't want your wound to get infected, then I'm going to have to clean it up," I explained.

"That's ridiculous," said Shaine. "I'm not bleeding and perfectly fine."

"Sire, the royal bottom *is* bleeding!" Flax pointed. Then Granate started laughing. "Why are you laughing?"

"You said royal bottom," Granate chuckled.

"Huh, I guess that is funny." Flax chuckled. Then Flax and Granate were both laughing. Shaine sighed and smacked his head.

"Look Shaine," I said, "right now you only have two options. Let me clean your wound up or let it get infected. So what do you say?"

From his pained look, he knew what had to be done.

— Chapter Twenty-Three —

Working Together

"This has to be the most embarrassing moment in my entire life," said Shaine.

The only thing he was wearing was a blanket that Flax held around him while I cleaned the arrow-stab in his butt with Granate's help.

"Wow, it didn't go as deep as I thought it did," I told him, "so this shouldn't take long. Then you can put your pants on."

"Thank goodness," Shaine mumbled.

"You know, this is kinda fun," admitted Granate.

"No, it's not," said Shaine and Flax at the same time. It was quiet for a moment. Then Flax spoke.

"You know your majesty," he said.

"Don't look at me," said Shaine, still embarrassed.

"Right, uhh," Flax paused. "Things could be a lot worse."

"How could anything else be worse than this?" Shaine asked.

"Oh, I know, I know." Granate put his hand up.

"Granate, put your hand down," I told him.

"Aww." Granate looked down.

"There, all done," I said. "You can put your pants on now." I threw him his pants and he put them on.

"Now that we're done with that," Flax walked away, "I'll go put this blanket back in the carriage and we can all go home."

"Oy, wait for me." Granate hurried to catch up with Flax.

"Hold on, I'm not finished with you two," said Shaine.

"Huh?" Flax and Granate stared at him in confusion.

"What are you two doing out here?" Shaine put his fists on his hips. "And don't say that it was my parents who sent you to spy on me."

"Isn't it obvious Shaine?" I spoke up. "They're out here because I escaped from the castle and came to capture me again."

"But you said you weren't from Chief Tinu's tribe," said Flax. I moved my hand across my neck to tell him to be quiet.

"Flax, even I knew Layla was saying that so the Dark Prince wouldn't suspect the real reason why we're out here," Granate explained.

Shaine turned his head to look at me and I put my hands behind my back and looked down. Then he looked back at Flax and Granate.

"Yeah, and she would have gotten away with it if you two didn't talk," said Shaine. "So what are you three really doing out here?"

Busted.

"So should I tell him, or do you guys want to go for it?" I asked.

Flax and Granate looked at each other. Then they put their heads down, looking guilty.

"We found a note that Princess Sylvia left behind," said Flax.

"It said that she was running away to Denna," Granate added.

"What?" Shaine looked surprised. "Why would she?" Shaine looked over at me, and understood what was going on. All I could do was stand there feeling guilty for letting this happen. My apology wasn't good enough. His hands gripped tighter. "He's with her isn't he? That scumbag is with her!" Then he ran off.

"Shaine!" I yelled. He couldn't hear me though. He was moving so fast that we almost couldn't see him anymore. "Come on." I jumped into the carriage. "We've got to catch up with him."

"Right." Flax and Granate got in the carriage too.

"Let's go," said Granate. Flax snapped the whip and we were moving. When we finally caught up with Shaine, we tried to keep the same pace as him.

"Shaine, where are you going?" I yelled.

"Where do you think I'm going?" Shaine shouted. "I'm going to Denna to get your dim-witted friend away from my fiancé."

"This is ridiculous!" I yelled. "Stop running away from us. We can't help you if you keep pushing us away."

"What's makes you think I need your help?" Shaine shouted.

"Because I know where they really are!" I hollered. Shaine stopped running and looked at me. Flax stopped the carriage and I got out.

"What do you mean you know where they really are?" Shaine asked.

"Knuckles also left a note for me," I explained. "And it said that he was running away with Princess Sylvia to Besha."

"Really?" Shaine looked interested.

"Yeah, but how do you know that Knuckles isn't tricking you?" Flax asked suspiciously.

"Because Knuckles couldn't make up a scheme if his life depended on it," I replied.

"And scheming something up is definitely the type of thing Sylvia likes to do," said Shaine.

"So we're going to Besha then?" Granate asked.

"Looks like it," said Flax.

"Then what are we standing around here for?" I said. "Let's get in the carriage and be on our way." I got in the carriage but noticed Shaine was giving me a weird look. "Oh, what's wrong now?"

"There's something weird about you," said Shaine.

"So, aren't we all weird to each other?" I asked.

"Yes, but there's something different about you," Shaine insisted. "You're strong, smart, and very stubborn when it comes to women's independence. You act more like an Overlander than an outcast."

"So I'm smarter than the other outcasts," I said. "Big deal. Can't one outcast like me be smarter than her or his tribe?" He thought about it for a minute.

"Hmm, I guess one or two can be smarter than their tribe," Shaine agreed. "But I don't know what I find the most interesting thing about you. The fact that you're more highly evolved than your tribe or the fact that Sora thought he could keep a secret from me on my own computer."

Crap.

"I don't understand," I lied nervously. "What does Sora keeping a secret from you have to do with me?"

"Save it, I already know he told you," said Shaine. "Once my brother finds something interesting about someone, he has to ask right away." Shaine put his hand in his pocket and held out a card. "I, on the other hand, like to keep it to myself until it's the right time to spill and tell."

It was one of the Royal Guards ID work passes. I remember someone complained about missing his card when Nilerm came to visit at the HQ Base. Shaine must have taken the card away from Nilerm when he was down here and inserted it into his Iden to get information about Overlanders. This means he knew who I really was now.

I glared at him. "Fine, you caught me." I admitted defeat, "Now what? You're going to kill me like your people have done to all the other Overlanders?"

"Overlander!" Flax and Granate yelped it out in unison. The carriage came to a stop.

"Quick, grab her!" shouted Flax.

"Oy!" shouted Granate.

As they grabbed me by the arms, I struggled to get out of their grip. If I was going to die, I wasn't going down without a fight for freedom.

"Let her go, guys," Shaine ordered.

"What?" Flax and Granate looked shocked.

"You heard me." Shaine jumped out of the carriage. "Let her go."

"But Dark Prince, she's an Overlander," said Flax, "And the law says ..."

"I am your future King," shouted Shaine. "Forget what the law says and do as I say. Let, her, go."

Flax and Granate looked at each other, not sure if he was being serious. Then they let go of me and got back in the carriage.

"You saved my life, I saved yours," said Shaine as he walked towards me and put out his hand. "We're even."

"Hmph," I mumbled as I got myself up. "And what about my friends?"

"They of course I will make no exception for." Shaine's face was cold. "Knuckles must be tried for his situation with Sylvia and the girl will be transferred to Sylvia's kingdom to work."

"Well you better hope that I don't run into them first," I warned him as I walked off.

"Oh I'm not worried about that at all," Shaine said with confidence. Then he used his super speed to grab me by the shoulders and pull me closer to him. "Because you're coming with us."

"What?" said Flax, Granate, and I.

"You didn't think that just because I spared your life I would let you leave freely did you?" Shaine smirked at me.

"Oh come on," I complained. "Look, if you're worried about me telling my King and Queen about this place then stop, because I promise by my heart I won't tell them anything."

"I won't have to worry about you telling them anything, because you'll never get to them," said Shaine. "Your family, your friends, will become memories as you will never see them again. There's only one route to the topside and it is impossible to get there."

"I've made it this far," I said. "Who says I couldn't get there?"

"Even if you did make it to the gateway, you don't get to decide what happens when you get there," said Shaine. "*It* decides what happens."

"It decides," I said confused. "What decides? What is it?"

"Well I could tell you but ...," said Shaine.

"But you're not going to tell me because you think it's pointless since you think I'll never make it there," I interrupted.

"Precisely," said Shaine. "If you want to live then you must stay down here or join your friends' fate. In all honesty, I think your best option is to stick with us." I growled at him.

"Oy, shall we get moving?" Granate asked softly.

"Yes, let's go," answered Shaine. He picked me up in his arms. "Try to keep up with me if you can." Flax and Granate smiled.

"Yes, Sire," they said.

With that said, Shaine ran at his super speed, with Flax and Granate following us as quickly as they could.

— Chapter Twenty-Four —

The Forbidden Jungle

"Whoa!" called out Shaine as he finally slowed and stopped. Once he came to a complete stop, he put me down. In front of us was another jungle.

"Sire, we're not going in there are we?" asked Granate.

"You're not," replied Shaine, "but I am."

"But your majesty, you can't go into the Forbidden Jungle," said Flax. "It's too dangerous."

"And it's the shortest way to Besha," said Shaine. "I'll be fine. I'll meet you two on the other side. And take Layla with you."

"What?" I stepped back. "No way. I'm going with you."

"I beg to differ," said Shaine.

"Hey, if this is the quickest way to Besha then I'm going with you," I told him. "Besides, not only will you not have to worry about me running off, but you'll also have someone watching your back in case you run into trouble."

"If anyone's going to run into trouble it will be you," said Shaine. "You don't know the Forbidden Jungle like I do."

"Well then, I guess you have a lot to teach me," I said as I walked by him and into the Forbidden Jungle. Before I actually went into the Forbidden Jungle though, I turned to look at him. "Don't worry, I'm a fast learner."

I could hear his growl as I continued to walk deeper into the Forbidden Jungle.

"Fine, you can come with me." Shaine caught up to me. "Just

do as I say and we'll get out of here safely." I rolled my eyes.

"Dark Prince, Dark Prince," shouted Flax.

"Wait for us," shouted Granate. They were trying to catch up with us. Shaine and I stopped walking.

"Flax, Granate," Shaine shouted, "I thought I told you two to take the long route and meet me on the other side with the carriage."

"Well, we were going to," said Granate, "but we thought it would be better if we stick together."

"Plus we still don't trust you completely," said Flax looking at me.

"Gee thanks," I said sarcastically.

"What did you do with the carriage?" Shaine asked.

"No need to worry about that," replied Flax as we continued to walk again. "I put on the ALE3000 auto-driver and hooked the reins to it. So it should be waiting for us on the other side by tomorrow."

"Perfect." Shaine smiled.

"ALE3000?" I asked confused.

"When you're too tired or just too lazy to drive, you attach the reins of the carriage to it and it drives for you."

First castles with weights and pools, now carriages with ALE3000 systems that drove carriages without a driver on-board. What was wrong with this place?

"Okay, now I know you're lying," I said.

"Excuse you!" Flax and Granate looked insulted.

"There is no such thing as this ALE3000 because not even Jurassic has something like that," I said.

"Just because it hasn't been invented in your hometown yet, doesn't mean it hasn't been invented in our hometown," said Granate.

"Yeah, who do you think you are, Miss I know everything?" Flax gave me a smug look.

"Says the reptiles who don't have cell phones or televisions,"

I said. They looked at each other confused. Then looked back at me.

"What are those?" asked Flax and Granate. I rolled my eyes and sighed.

"My point ex ... ," I said.

"Shhh," hissed Shaine.

"Did you just ... ?" I said.

"Shhh," Shaine lifted a hand for emphasis.

"I think he did just ... ," Granate whispered.

"Shhh," hissed Shaine.

"Will you two ... ," Flax whispered.

"Shhh!" Shaine hissed louder, glaring now. "Quiet!"

Suddenly, we heard an animal growling. It was moving closer, getting louder and louder until the bushes moved.

"Rrruuff!"

"Monster!" screamed Flax and Granate and turned to run.

"Everybody run," shouted Shaine as we ran away from the animal. As we ran for it, I could hear the animal jumping out of the bushes.

"Rrruuff!" roared the monster again.

"Ahh!" I screamed as I hit the ground and went into the protection position. But as the monster leaped towards me, something pulled it back.

"Ruff" whined the monster and I heard frantic scrabbling behind me.

"Huh," I said.

I walked over and peered through the bushes. The monster had been dragged down into a huge, deep hole. Huge tree roots protruded from the sides of the pit. I took a closer look at the monster and saw that it was no monster. It was a puppy. A purple puppy. The poor thing was trying to get out of the hole, but it was caught on a branch.

The puppy whined more loudly.

"Hang on, I'm coming," I shouted.

The puppy barked, trying to run up the sides of the pit to me.

As I made it halfway down, Shaine appeared at the top. "Layla, get back up here!"

"I will as soon as I help that puppy out," I said.

"Layla no!" Shaine yelled. Then, with an echo of the yell in his sigh, he came down after me. "Stubborn girl."

"Sire, wait for us." Flax and Granate were sliding down, too. "We'll help you," said Granate. Close to the ground, I jumped off and ran to the puppy.

"Layla, leave the puppy alone," yelled Shaine.

"And let the poor thing get eaten by some other wild animal?" I said. "No way." I crouched down to the puppy and started to free it from the branch that held it.

"If you set that mutt free then we'll all end up as dinner." Shaine jumped the rest of the way into the pit and ran to me. Flax and Granate tried the same move, but they fell on their faces. I had already set the puppy free. I picked it up and stood back up.

The puppy barked and licked my face. I giggled.

"This is not good," Shaine said grimly.

"I think I just coughed up my tailbone," said Flax as he and Granate joined us.

"Ouch," moaned Granate. Suddenly a loud roar shook the ground.

"What was that?" I asked. The roaring stopped. It was silent. Shaine was looking around.

"Everyone climb up!" he ordered. Then a bunch of branches swooped down from the trees surrounding the hole to strike at us. "Quickly!"

Flax and Granate screamed in unison.

With Flax and Granate still screaming, we ran to the walls and climbed. I couldn't believe I was running away from moving branches. How was that even possible?

"Watch out for the tree roots," Shaine warned us. "They'll

grab you by the leg and drag you down to the trees' mouths."

Trees' mouths? As I followed with the puppy, a branch popped out when I reached for a handhold. I held on to the branch and pulled myself up. Once I was away from the branch, I continued to climb. "Any more surprises?" Suddenly, a huge tree root burst through the side of the pit under my feet and started to push me back to the floor. The puppy jumped onto a perch on the pit wall. "Whoa!"

The puppy barked frantically. Shaine turned back and saw me.

"Layla!"

He was climbing down to rescue me. Was he ever going to learn? Since the root hadn't actually wrapped around my legs yet, I just needed to figure out how to get back to the wall. Then on the other side of the pit, another huge root popped out of the wall and swung over towards me. When the huge root was right over me, I jumped up, grabbed onto the root, and swung myself up and over the top of it.

"Whew," I gasped.

"Layla," Shaine called.

I looked over to see that the root was swinging me towards him, and he was holding out his hand, from where he clung to the wall. When he was close enough, I grabbed his hand and he pulled me up. Roots were starting to pop out everywhere.

"Oh," I said as Shaine and I ducked.

The puppy barked again.

"Hurry, we have to keep climbing," said Shaine.

"Right," I said. "Come here, puppy."

The puppy barked as he jumped into my arms. The root was going to grab us, but we jumped to another root just in time to get away.

"Don't worry, your majesty," shouted Granate, still climbing to the top.

"We'll get you two out of there," shouted Flax.

"Flax, Granate, watch out!" Shaine yelled.

They both looked back up. Six huge roots studded with thorns appeared right in front of them. They smacked Flax and Granate, who let go of the wall and fell, screaming.

"Granate, Flax!" I shouted. As they fell past us, a root thrust out from the pit wall beneath them, catching them.

"Ouch," said Granate.

"That hurt," said Flax.

The roots were going crazy. They kept thrusting across the pit everywhere, but we all kept jumping from one root to another.

"Now what?" I asked Shaine.

"Oh, *now* you want to listen to me?" Shaine looked around and pointed. "There."

I looked up. "Those vines?"

"Flax, Granate," shouted Shaine, "go to the vines."

They did as they were told and made their way to the vines. Shaine swooped me into his arms and jumped root to root until we reached the vines. Slowly and steadily, I started to climb.

"Don't climb," said Shaine.

"Are you kidding," I said. "If we stay here the roots will tear us apart."

"And if you climb up, the thorns will stab you to death," Shaine pointed out. I looked at the pointy thorns on the roots above and remembered what had happened to Flax and Granate.

"Well what are we supposed to do?" I asked.

"Just stay put," said Shaine. "Got it, guys?"

"Got it," said Flax and Granate.

The roots were going crazy now. They were slashing each other, moving in and out of the walls. They were also moving faster, as if the trees were getting ticked off, trying to catch us. They were getting closer. The vines were lowering us down to the furious roots.

The puppy whined.

"Now what?" I asked nervously.

"Wait for it," Shaine said smoothly. Everything was closing in on us. I thought we were going to die. That was until a root studded with thorns slammed into the vines. "Hang on." Without a warning, the vines yanked us straight up.

The puppy yelped.

"Whoa!" I shouted.

Flax and Granate screamed. Once we were out of that trap hole, the vines swung us in a short arc and suddenly we were all flying straight up through the air.

"Wahoo!" Shaine yelled with glee.

"Oh my gosh!" I yelled back. "We're gonna die."

"Don't worry," shouted Granate as he flapped his arms, "Just think of happy things and then you can fly."

"That doesn't work, you fool," said Flax. "Besides, you need pixie dust, too, in order to fly."

"Do we even have fairies around here?" Granate asked.

"Not that I know of," replied Flax. We came to the point where our rapid ascent slowed and we paused in mid-air. Then gravity went back to work.

Everyone screamed. We hit a couple of the trees' vines and small branches, but the thickly matted vines saved our fall. We bounced and finally stopped moving, hanging in vines above the ground.

"Is everyone alright?" asked Shaine as we struggled in the vines.

The puppy barked and wagged his tail.

"I'm fine," I said.

"I'm okay," said Granate.

"So what's the plan now?" asked Flax as he tried to untangle himself. Shaine had freed himself from the vines and was sitting on a tree limb.

"Get down and keep moving," Shaine told him.

While he was climbing down the tree, the rest of us were trying to get untangled from the vines. The problem for me though, was that I had a puppy on top of me. Since I was pretty close to the tree, I swung myself back and forth until the puppy could jump to the tree.

When the puppy was off me, I untangled myself while swinging from the vine and jumped onto the tree. I turned around to see Flax and Granate still trying to get untangled from the vines. I leaned my hand on the tree and my other hand on my hip.

"Are you two coming or what?" I asked.

"Yes," answered Granate, "just as soon as we get out ... "

"Granate, watch out!" Flax warned him.

But it was too late. Granate bumped into Flax and now they were tangled together with Flax upside down.

"It could be worse," Granate pointed out.

"I doubt that," Flax disagreed. There was a popping sound. The vines broke and they were falling.

They bounced off a few branches before they fell to the ground.

"Are you two alright?" I yelled.

"We're fine," said Flax painfully as Granate groaned.

Now that everyone was out of the vines, I grabbed the puppy and started to climb down the tree.

— Chapter Twenty-Five —

It's a Cookie

"Took you long enough," Granate called out.

"Hey, I had a passenger to help," I called back. Safe on the ground, the puppy started licking my face, making me laugh. "That tickles."

"It's a cookie," said Granate.

"*This* is a cookie?" I held the cookie away from me to get a better look at it.

"Yup, that's a cookie, alright," replied Flax. "One of the cutest things you'll ever see in the Forbidden Jungle."

He was right, it was really cute. For a purple little alien dog thing, that is. The puppy's eyes were yellow; even its pupils were a dark yellow, like amber. It had one huge black spot on its back and pink on the tip of its pointy ears and a little bit of pink on its front paws.

"If you're done with your distractions," said Shaine, "let's keep moving." With that said, we followed him and continued walking.

"So what are you going to name the cookie?" asked Granate.

"Hmm ... let's see," I put the cookie down to take a good look at it. Its eyes glowed in the shadows, but in the light they sparkled brighter than a star. "I've got it, I'll call this cookie Sparkles."

"Sparkles?" Flax and Granate looked shocked.

"Yeah, Sparkles."

"You can't name the cookie Sparkles," said Flax.

"Why not?" I asked.

"Because it's a boy." Granate looked down his nose at me.

"So?" I shrugged "You can name a boy or girl Sparkles."

"But it sounds weird," said Flax.

"Well *I* think Sparkles suits him," said Granate.

"Thank you, Granate," I said.

Sparkles barked.

"Whoa, whoa, whoa." Shaine stopped walking. He turned around and looked at me. "You did not just say what I think you said."

"Yes, I'm keeping the cookie," I said.

"No. That creature is not coming with us," said Shaine.

"Well I'm not leaving the poor thing on its own," I said. "So he comes with us."

"No he won't," said Shaine.

"Yes he will," I said.

"The mutt goes," said Shaine.

"The cookie stays," I said.

"Can I say something?" Granate raised his hand.

"No!" Shaine and I yelled. Granate kept quiet and he and Flax watched us.

"Fine. The cookie can come with us," Shaine finally agreed. "I don't have time to argue with you. Just watch him and stay out of trouble. Unless you decide not to listen to me again, especially when I've been here more than any of you." Angry, Shaine stormed off.

"Dark Prince, wait." Granate ran to catch up with him.

"*We* are listening to you." Flax followed. What had I done? I sighed.

"Come on, Sparkles," I said. "We've got a long road ahead of us."

Sparkles barked and we hurried to catch up with the others.

Once again, we had another hill to climb. Only this one was longer and steeper.

"So why are these little guys called cookies?" I asked Flax and Granate.

"Because cookies are the only thing that they eat," Granate explained.

"Really?" I said, amazed.

"Well they also drink milk," Flax added, "but only if they have a cookie with it."

"And where do they get the cookies from?" I didn't believe him for a minute. "It's not like they can grow on trees."

"Yes they do." Flax sounded surprised. "It's called a Cookie Tree. It's also where the milk comes from."

"What? How is that possible?" I said in disbelief. "How does a tree make milk?"

"During a rainstorm, the tree sucks up the water with it roots," Flax explained, "and when the water mixes with the special chemical substance inside it; it produces milk."

"So all the cookie has to do is bite a hole in the tree and it drinks the milk," Granate added.

"Of course," I laughed.

"Don't you have cookie trees?" Granate asked.

"No, we have cows and baking ingredients to produce milk and cookies," I answered.

Flax and Granate looked at me, puzzled.

"Cows?" Flax blinked.

"What's a cow?" Granate scratched his head.

I sighed. Sparkles barked. We looked up at Shaine who was way ahead of us.

"You think the Dark Prince is still mad at us?" asked Granate.

"Of course he is," Flax answered, "and I don't blame him. He has the right to be mad at all of us." Then he pointed his finger at me. "Especially you."

"Me?" I frowned at them. "I just said the cookie is mine and is coming with us. He doesn't have to get so overdramatic about it."

"It's more than that," said Flax. "When we came with him in the Forbidden Jungle, all he asked from us was that we listen to him, because as our leader and soon to become King of Owashia, he cares about our protection. But we didn't listen to him when he told us not to come with him, you didn't listen to him when he said not to go after that cookie, and when he said not to bring the cookie along."

"Oh, I feel horrible." Granate looked as if he was about to cry. "When we don't listen to him, what kind of respect are we showing the Dark Prince? How can he protect his people when we don't give him the respect he deserves?"

Flax and Granate were right on that one. When you don't listen to your rulers, you put disgrace on a King and Queen's honour, especially regarding safety matters. There was a moment of silence.

"So who wants to go apologize?" Flax spoke.

Since Flax had asked, it was obvious he didn't want to do it. Granate was too terrified to go do it. Heck, he looked like he was about ready to have a heart attack. I rolled my eyes at them.

"I'll do it." I broke into a trot to catch up with Shaine.

Shaine was right. I was wrong. Even though he knew this place was dangerous, he'd let us come anyway. All he'd asked in return was for us to listen to him. When the time came, I didn't listen to him and almost got us all killed. And having Sparkles along with us showed that I didn't respect him as a leader or a prince, which brought disgrace and embarrassment to him in front of his people. Even though it was only Flax and Granate that were here with him. Heck, Shaine had been born in this underground world so he *did* know it better than I did. I needed to take a step down and let him lead. I mean, if I wanted to make peace between our worlds, this would be a good opportunity to get on the Dark Prince's good side.

"Shaine," I began.

"What do you want now?" He didn't look at me.

"Look, you can be mad at me as long as you like," I told him, "but don't take it out on Flax and Granate. I'm the one that disrespected you, not them. And I'm sorry that I ... "

"What did you say?" Shaine interrupted.

"I said you could be ... "

"No, after that?"

"I said I'm sorry," I said tentatively.

He stopped climbing and looked away from me. I stopped climbing and waited for him to say something. But he was as stiff and silent as a rock.

"Shaine," I whispered softly. He still stood there like a rock. Then he looked back at me and smiled.

"It's not completely your fault," said Shaine as we continued to climb. "Almost getting us killed, that was your fault. But bringing the cookie with us, I might have overreacted a little bit." I stared at him.

"Might, a little bit," I said.

"Okay, I did overreact." Shaine smiled again. "Let's just forget that this ever happened and move on." He paused for a moment. "Although next time you see another animal in trouble, please just leave it alone and let the circle of life do its job." I couldn't help but giggle at that comment.

"Okay, you've got yourself a deal," I said as we shook hands. He looked at me and sighed.

"It's alright guys, I'm not mad at you," Shaine told them. "You can move faster now."

Flax and Granate did as he said and climbed faster. He looked at his watch and then we continued to climb. "Once we all get to the top, we can take a breather for awhile before we start going down."

"I don't suppose that watch of yours also happens to be a tracking device?" I asked curiously.

"Tracking device?" Shaine turned to look at me. "Why would I want to track animal prints?"

"No, that's not what I meant," I said. He was still looking at me, confused. Then he must have remembered something.

"Oh, you mean one of those computer chips that you put on someone so that you can keep track of them wherever they are?" Shaine nodded. "I wish, but we don't have those yet."

"Look, I hope you don't mind me asking," I said, "but what year is this? I'm really confused here. You have people that dress and act like they're in the 17th century, but then you have other people that dress and act like a bunch of caveman. As for the things you own, your watch, workout equipment, and pool were not invented when castles and carriages were around. And that ALE ... ."

"It's called the Lost Time," Shaine said slowly.

— Chapter Twenty-Six —

Lost Time

"Lost Time?" I said interested.

"The Lost Time is its own timeline," Shaine explained. "You can find things here from any timeline the Lost Time chooses. It can come from any year in the world's timeline. That's why everything is the way it is, including the people."

"I'm not sure if I completely believe that," I told him. "The gadgets I believe, but the people? "The only people I've seen are people from the past—that would be the outcasts—and the present. That's you and your brothers I guess. Where's the future?"

"Oh they're around." Shaine smirked. "In fact, you've already met two people from your world's future."

"Really," I said, "Who?"

"Oy, get away from me," shouted Flax. I slowly turned around.

"Oy, cut it out Flax," said Granate. "He just wants to play."

"Yeah, well I don't want to play," said Flax, "I want to get to the top."

Sparkles was chewing on a sturdy vine that Flax was using to climb up the steep slope. The vine broke and Flax went rolling down the hill.

"Hahahaha!" laughed Granate as Flax hollered. Once Flax stopped rolling, he climbed back up to where Granate was still chuckling.

"Oh you think that's funny?" said Flax. "Well laugh at this." Flax pulled Granate's tail and they both went rolling down the hill, wrestling each other.

Sparkles barked madly. I looked back at Shaine.

"You mean we're gonna ... ," I said quickly. He smiled.

"You didn't think we'd be pure humans forever, did you?"

He looked away from me and hmmed. "That's what makes this place different from your world above. The one thing that you Overlanders stop believing in when you grow up."

"Oh," I said, "and what's that?"

"Magic, Layla," said Shaine, "magic."

Magic. They all believed in magic. The last time I believed in or even thought about magic was when I was eight. When Shaine and I made it to the top, he held out his hand. There was that tingly feeling again as I grabbed his hand and he pulled me up. As he pulled me up though, I tripped over a rock.

"Whoa." I flailed my arms for balance.

"Gotcha." Shaine caught me.

I got myself back up still holding on to him. We were in the same position as at the castle, only this time he had his hands on my hips. We looked into each other's eyes. The wind swirled around us. I felt my face flushing. What was going on with me?

"Ouch!" we heard Granate shout as Shaine and I came back to reality. "That hurt."

"You asked for it!" shouted Flax.

Sparkles was barking.

"Flax, Granate, knock it off," yelled Shaine. Flax and Granate stopped wresting "We still have a long way to go before we get to our destination."

"Sparks, come here boy," I shouted.

Sparkles barked as he obeyed and we started climbing up the hill.

"Coming," said Flax and Granate as they let go of each other and went back to climbing.

Well, from what I'd seen of this underground world, I would believe that magic does rule this place. While we waited for them, I heard a strange noise from behind. It sounded like a little critter. I turned my head around, but there was nothing there. I heard the noise again and looked to the left. Still nothing. I heard the noise again. This time I looked to the right and saw something. Glowing green eyes gleamed in the tree and then disappeared.

"Shaine," I whispered.

"What is it?" Shaine was too busy watching Flax and Granate climbing up. Then a couple of more glowing green eyes appeared and the noise got louder.

"I think we're being watched," I told him.

"By who, the trees again?" Shaine wasn't really listening.

"Only if they have glowing green eyes," I said.

"Glowing green eyes?" Shaine frowned. He stepped in front of me and the glowing green eyes flashed and disappeared. He looked side to side. "Stay behind me."

Moving further into the jungle, I noticed a green X on the ground and heard a giggle coming from the trees. It was a trap.

"What the ... ?" Shaine looked around, clearly wondering who was giggling.

"Shaine, watch out," I said as I pulled him back. "It's a trap." I pointed at the X.

"Good call," said Shaine. "Let's head back, quickly." Suddenly there was a roaring laugh.

"Smart girl isn't she," said a familiar voice. "That's why I put the trap in front of the X." As another laugh roared out, the ground gave way under our feet and we fell down a hole and onto a slide.

Shaine and I both yelled as we slid downward, picking up speed. At the end, we shot up into the air and went tumbling down onto dirt. We kept rolling until we came to a complete stop.

"Ouch," I mumbled.

"Layla," said Shaine. He got on his feet and ran over to me.

"You okay?"

"I'm fine," I replied. I was surprised that we didn't have any broken bones or bruises. Or bleeding for that matter. "Are you alright?"

"I'm fine," said Shaine.

We were in another pit except that the walls were all rock instead of dirt. In front of us was a cave big enough for a giant to stand up in.

"Sire!" shouted Flax from above.

"Are you two alright?" shouted Granate.

"We're fine, guys." said Shaine. We were both back on our feet now. "Just take Sparkles with you and keep moving. We'll be right behind you, once we climb back up."

As Flax, Granate, and Sparkles left, we heard a low, deep, growl. Shaine and I slowly turned toward the cave. There were glowing, green eyes inside.

"Shaine," I whispered, "What is that?"

"Animal abuse," said Shaine in anger.

"Oh come now, Shaine," said the familiar voice again from above. "What you call abusive ..." Chief Tinu's tribal symbol appeared above the animal eyes. "I call fun. I thought you, the Dark Prince of people, would think the same." Oh great, we meet Chief Tinu's oldest son Clint again. My skin crawled.

"Animals are innocent creatures that live here and kill for their survival," said Shaine. "Not your toys that you can play with anytime you want." The animal made a whimpering growl.

"I beg to differ," said the voice.

"What do you want, Clint?" asked Shaine.

"I'm here to speak with my bride to be," said Clint.

It looked like I was dealing with a guy that couldn't take no for an answer.

"My love, I'm giving you another chance to decide. Marry me and become Queen of my tribe, or live with the con ... con ...."

"Consequences." Shaine spoke wearily.

"Yes, conquencis," said Chief Tinu's son.

Oh brother.

"So what do you say, my pet?"

"My answer is still no," I said. "I could never be with a guy who's going to treat me like an animal."

"You're making a big mistake," Clint warned me.

"I'm willing to take my chances," I told him.

"You heard the little ... ," said Shaine before he looked at me. He saw my glare at what he was about to say, coughed, and started his sentence again. "You heard her." The animal growled louder with Clint's anger. Then it whined.

"Oh, now I understand," said Clint. "You can't marry me because you're engaged to the Dark Prince."

Engaged! "No, we're just friends," I said.

"No, we're not a couple," said Shaine at the same time.

"Now, now, dear, there's no need to hide it." Clint's tone was saccharine. "I can see the love. But if there's ever going to be an 'us,' then there's only one solution."

The animal came out of its cave. Shaine and I slowly backed away from the creature, but it kept moving towards us. This animal was horrifying. It was a combination of two mythical creatures that I would never have even thought of, a hunched over werewolf that was part centaur.

— Chapter Twenty-Seven —

Where's the Tartar Sauce?

"Any last words?" Clint asked, amused.

"Yeah, I do," said Shaine. He pointed to the right. "Is that Shamu eating all your sour keys over there?"

"What!" said Clint, shocked. The werewolf-centaur looked to the right.

"Come on," whispered Shaine. We made a run for it in the opposite direction and started climbing up the rocks.

"How can you see that far?" Clint asked amazed and annoyed. "I'm using this creature's eyes and I can't even ...." He turned the creature back to us, but we weren't there. He looked around until he spied us at the top of the slide.

"Run!" shouted Shaine as we ran for our lives.

"Get back here and face your fate, Dark Prince!" screamed Clint.

The werewolf-centaur was coming after us. It was getting closer and closer. We were doomed. Shaine stopped running in front of a tree with roots arching from the ground that form a sort of cave.

"Quick, get under the roots and we'll make our escape," said Shaine. He went under the roots and put out his hand.

"You promise there won't be any more roots attacking us?" I asked.

"Trust me," said Shaine.

I grabbed his hand and he dragged me under the roots. As

we crawled beneath them to get to the other side, the werewolf-centaur crashed headlong into the tree. Shaine had managed to get out, but at the werewolf-centaur's impact, the roots caged me in like a tiger in a circus.

"Shaine!" I screamed and he looked back.

"Layla!" Shaine shouted as he ran back to help me. The werewolf-centaur had fallen, dazed, to its knees. "Can you get out of there?"

"I think so," I said. "I just need a little more space." I pushed the roots as Shaine pulled them.

"You stupid animal!" Clint shouted. He must have been hurting the poor creature, because it was moaning in pain.

Finally, it opened its eyes and saw us.

"Quick, grab the girl and then kill him!" ordered Clint. The werewolf-centaur stretched its werewolf torso partway under the tree and used its big, clawed hand to grab me.

I kicked at it and it let go.

Shaine had a tight hold of my hand and was pulling, but the roots still blocked me.

"Come on you stupid creature!" yelled Clint, "Grab her!"

It tried again, but its claws snagged on the roots and actually pulled them away from me. Shaine pulled me out and we ran. The werewolf-centaur roared after us, but the tree broke suddenly and fell on it.

The last thing I heard from Clint was, "Come on you waste of space, get out of there and after them,"

Climbing up another hill, we came panting to the top. Coming out of the jungle, we found open space from here on, but at least we weren't being followed by that werewolf-centaur or whatever they called it down here. No trees, no vines, no bushes, nothing. The rest of the jungle was on the other side of the gravelly landscape. Halfway across the rocky grounds, we came to a drop.

"Whoa," I said as I skidded to a stop. Little pieces of rock beneath my feet tumbled down into the crevasse. It looked like a hundred, two hundred foot drop.

"Looks like a dead end." Shaine came up behind me. We heard a roar from the jungle, behind us.

"Now what?" I asked. "That tree won't hold the animal for long. And he'll see us out on this open ground."

"Hold on," said Shaine. He looked around. "Layla, over here." I dropped to the ground on my knees and saw a round, smooth stone that had markings like the layout of a maze.

"How is this going to help us?" I asked.

"Simple," said Shaine, "we put our hand on this gravity stone and bring up some rocks. Once we get enough floating rocks lined up to make a bridge, we'll cross over to the other side and make our escape." I looked at him like he was a psycho.

"Floating rocks?" I could feel my eyebrows rising. "You can't be serious."

"You have to believe in the power of magic, Layla," Shaine told me. "If you don't, it's the end of our lives."

"Okay, okay, I'll try," I said.

With that said we put our hands on the stone and concentrated on lifting rocks. It shouldn't be hard to do, I told myself. I just had to believe in the magic like when I was five. I kept telling myself that I could do it over and over again, with my eyes closed, visualizing those rocks rising from the bottom of the crevasse, locking together to form a bridge ….

"We did it," said Shaine.

I opened my eyes and saw a bunch of floating rocks making a path in the air for us to the other side. I smiled with delight. Magic really *did* exist down here. We heard another angry roar coming from the forest.

"Let's get out of here." I ran onto the floating rocks.

"Layla, slow down!" Shaine shouted as he tried to catch up with me. When I stopped running, the rock I was on literally swerved to the left.

"Whoa!" I yelped, wavering. I thought I was going to fall. Luckily, Shaine caught my arm and pulled me back. We steadily jumped to the next rock and continued to walk across our floating path.

"Just because these rocks are floating tightly together, doesn't mean they're stable," said Shaine. "Move slow and steady and we'll be on the other side in no time." We stopped walking when we heard the werewolf-centaur roar again, along with the sound of trees crashing down. "Okay, change of plans, move more swiftly."

We ran for it. Halfway to the other side, the stomp of the centaur hooves vibrated through the ground making the rocks rise and fall. The vibration made them become unstable in the air and they started falling into the crevasse again.

I screamed as the rocks between me and the far side began to drop away. Shaine stepped up beside me and pulled me into his chest. I held on to him as tightly as I could. The werewolf-centaur had seen us and was coming after us.

"Layla, remember when you asked me how I disappeared from that fight with your friend?" asked Shaine.

"Yeah," I answered. He took out a small, green rock.

"Well you're about to find out," he told me. The werewolf-centaur jumped onto the floating rocks. The rocks couldn't take the animal's weight and we were all falling now as he galloped toward us. He put out his paw to grab us. I closed my eyes and squeezed Shaine. "Chaos freeze!" Shaine said in a quiet, firm voice.

Through my closed eyelids, I saw a flash of light. I opened my eyes. I couldn't believe what I was seeing. Time had frozen around us. The rocks went down slowly; even the werewolf-centaur was reaching for us very slowly.

"There." Shaine pointed to a rock. The rock was not rounded like the others; it was flat. "If we get on that rock, the weretar will pass us and we should have a bit of a soft landing ... I think."

"Is that what it's called?" I asked.

"Yup," Shaine answered.

I was trying my best to get to the rock as we sank down, but it was really hard to do. Luckily, Shaine knew what he was doing. Time was starting to come back to normal and the rocks were going down faster.

"We're running out of time!" shouted Shaine. He gave me a push and I was on the rock. Time speeded up to normal and the weretar snatched him.

"Shaine!" I screamed.

I couldn't see if he got away. All the rocks were swirling all over the place. Another rock was going to ram into me if I didn't move. Thinking quickly, I leaped off into the trees. The two rocks smacked into each other and pieces went everywhere. I hit a few branches until I finally clawed my way onto a firm branch.

"Oww." I tried to get my breath back and heard the weretar growl.

I looked down to see that it had survived the fall! Wow! It looked all around and then took off. I didn't see Shaine with the animal. What if it had killed him? I scrambled down from the tree and started looking for him. Suddenly I heard barking.

"Sparkles!" I called out. The barking got louder. Sparkles appeared and leaped into my arms, licking my face. "Calm down, boy, I'm alright. Now where's Flax and Granate?" Sparkles stopped licking my face and looked behind him. Then he looked at me and whined. He seemed sad to have let me down.

"It's okay boy," I told him. "They can't be that far, we'll find them later." I put Sparkles down and saw something. Hanging in the bushes was Shaine's watch. "Oh my gosh. Sparkles! Come here boy." He did as he was told and came to me. I showed him the watch. "Think you can find Shaine with this?" Sparkles sniffed. Then he barked and clearly started following a scent.

"Good boy," I said. It took Sparkles about a minute to find him.

He stood over him and barked until I got there.

"Oh no," I gasped. There he was on the ground, at the base of a tree, with cuts everywhere on his body.

"Shaine!" I ran over to him. "Sparkles, go find Flax and Granate and bring them over here."

Sparkles barked and tore off to find them. I lay down beside Shaine and gently held his face.

"Shaine, wake up." I was feeling panicky. "The weretar is gone, you can stop pretending now." But he didn't respond. "Come on, please wake up." Not even a blink to show that he was okay. I put two fingers on his neck. No pulse. I put my head against his chest and let the tears come. He was dead. And there was nothing I could do.

"You idiot," I cried, "Why did you go and get yourself killed. You're the only one that knows everything about this place. We need you. *I* need you."

My heart felt like it had shattered into a million pieces. Like I'd lost a part of me now that Shaine was gone. Why was I getting so upset about this? I mean I did care about him a lot but … the way that I was feeling right now … gosh, why wouldn't this feeling go away? Then suddenly, I felt his chest rise and fall. He was breathing. He was alive.

"Ugh." Shaine breathed out. "When I run into Clint … I'm gonna … kill him."

"Shaine, you're alive." I hugged him.

"What was I before?" Shaine blinked at me, confused. "Ouch!"

"Oh, I'm sorry." I let go of him. "Oh Shaine, I'm glad that you're alright. I was so … "

"Worried?" Shaine said with a smirk on his face. I frowned at him and then turned away.

"Yeah right," I lied. "So what was that small green rock you used to slow down time?"

"It's called a timestone," said Shaine. "I found it up in the cold snowy mountains in a mysterious cave I discovered. Legend behind it says that you can control time and space with this stone, as you saw yourself. This is the only timestone. I thought it was just a myth. Never in my mind did I ever think I would find it."

"Guess it must have been fate for you to find it," I said.

Shaine smiled at me. Then he looked at the timestone. "Yeah, I guess so," he said.

I heard Sparkles bark.

"Sire, Layla?" shouted Flax.

"Are you alright?" shouted Granate.

"I'm fine," I said, "Shaine, on the other hand, could use some first aid."

"Oy, you can say that again," said Granate as the pair ran up to us.

"I don't need first aid, I'm fine," said Shaine. But as soon as he got up, the pain of his injuries hit him and his knees buckled. I caught him just in time, before he hit the ground.

"You sure?" I asked, keeping him balanced.

"Yeah," said Shaine. We looked into each other's eyes and smiled.

"Don't worry your majesty." Flax picked up Shaine and slung him gently over his shoulders. "Once we get to the carriage, we'll have those cuts healed up in no time."

"And how long is it going to take to get to the carriage?" I asked.

"Uhh ... probably the whole day," Granate answered.

"We can't wait that long," I said. "Shaine's got some serious injuries and they need to be dealt with ASAP."

"Don't worry, I'll be fine," said Shaine. "Besides, if we keep going on this route, we'll run into some gooble trees."

"Gooble trees?" I asked curiously.

"It's a special kind of healing tree that grows in all our regions," Shaine explained.

"Huh, interesting," I said. "Is there anything that you don't know about this place?"

"Just how the animals got their names," said Shaine. "Flax and Granate's ancestors named them all. Right boys?"

"Right," Flax and Granate said in perfect unison.

"Oh," I said, "so how did your ancestors come up with the name weretar?"

"Layla, Layla, Layla." Shaine shook his head. "You of all people I thought would have guessed that. It's the combination of the names werewolf and centaur."

"Shaine, Shaine, Shaine," I said as I shook my head at him. "You poor little boy. You of all people should know better."

"Hmm, that's a good guess Sire," said Flax.

"I would have never thought of it that way," said Granate.

"Wait you mean your ancestors didn't call it a weretar because it's part werewolf part centaur?" asked Shaine.

"Nope." Flax and Granate both shook their heads.

"If that's not the reason, then why do you call it a weretar?" asked Shaine. Flax and Granate looked at each other. Then they looked away and shrugged.

"Where's the tartar sauce?" Granate said hesitantly.

Oh boy.

"Aww, my head," said Shaine obviously wishing he'd never asked. I giggled.

"Take a deep breath your majesty," I told him, "we have a long way to go."

— Chapter Twenty-Eight —

Lizard Tribe

"Are we getting any closer to these gooble trees?" I asked.

"We should have passed by some twenty minutes ago," Shaine said concerned. "Flax, Granate, where have you taken us?"

"I don't know Sire," said Flax.

"We followed your orders," said Granate.

"Well we better find out before we run into any more trouble," I said calmly.

"Right," agreed Shaine. "Just put me down and I'll get us out of here."

"No can do Sire," said Granate.

"It's for your own good," said Flax.

Sparkles barked as he ran ahead us. He stopped suddenly and ran into the bushes.

"What's his problem?" asked Granate.

"Maybe he knows that we didn't share the cookies that we had with him," whispered Flax.

"Or maybe he found some gooble trees," I suggested.

I went ahead of them and ran after Sparkles. Flax and Granate followed behind. When we caught up with Sparkles, no cookies or gooble trees. There were no trees at all anymore, just huts in a huge circle. In the middle was a big bonfire that hadn't burned out yet.

"Here," said Flax as put down Shaine, "hold on to the Dark Prince." I held Shaine around his waist while he leaned on me with his arms around my shoulders. Flax took out a piece of paper and unfolded it.

"There's no village on the map," said Granate.

"There aren't any communities at all on the map," said Flax.

"How can you two have a map of the Forbidden Jungle?" asked Shaine. "Nobody besides me has gotten out alive to even make a map."

"Well if it isn't a map." Flax smirked as he handed it over. "Then what is it?" I looked at the piece of paper.

"It's a badly drawn map that someone coloured with crayons," I said. Flax and Granate took a better look at the so-called map. Then they looked at each other.

"Huh, what do you know," said Granate, "it is a badly drawn out map." Flax put the paper back in his pocket.

"So, if we're in a tribe's territory right now," said Flax, "then where is everybody?"

"I don't know," replied Shaine, "but I don't want to stick around to find out."

"Agreed," I said. Suddenly, a bunch of humanoid lizards appeared behind us, pointing their spears.

We were surrounded and they started herding us over to the bonfire.

"Hands up," said one of the humanoid lizards and we did as we were told.

"Listen, we mean you no harm," I told them. "My friend here is injured and we were just looking for some gooble trees to help heal him, but we got lost along the way." The lizard leader poked his spear closer to my neck.

"Why should we believe anything you have to say?" he asked.

"Hue," said Granate.

"Granate, is that you?" The lizard pulled the spear back from my neck.

"Yes it is." Granate was grinning.

"And Flax," added Flax.

"Eh, welcome back, boys." Hue passed by me and went to greet Flax and Granate. Soon every lizard humanoid had come over to Flax and Granate, welcoming them home.

"Granate, Flax, you know them?" asked Shaine.

"Yeah, this is our herd," replied Granate.

"You know, before we moved into Owashia and joined you, Dark Prince," Flax added. Granate's eyes opened wide and he looked around, puzzled.

"Oy, where's Charmey?" he asked. Flax shrugged.

"Ahh, Flax and Granate," said a voice from the far back.

Everyone moved to the side, giving us a clear view of the person who had spoken. He wasn't like Flax or Granate, or any of the other humanoid lizards who reminded me of Komodo Dragons. He was more like a chameleon. He had the normal green skin colour for any chameleon and his eyes popped out. Literally. Even though he was looking at us, his eyes seemed to go everywhere. Up, down, left, right, even in a circle. He wore a long, brown, hooded sweater and used a wooden cane as he limped over to us.

"I haven't seen you two for a very long time." He smiled at Flax and Granate.

"Hello Mister Charmey," Granate greeted him.

"So how are things going with you, Flax and Granate?" asked Charmey.

"Well right now, not so good," Granate answered.

"You see, our King the Dark Prince ran into a weretar and is hurt," explained Flax.

"A weretar you say, eh," said Charmey as he rubbed his chin. "That's quite serious."

"Do you have any gooble goo we can use?" asked Granate.

"Oh yes, of course we do," said Charmey. He pointed at two lizard men. "You two, bring the bedrock." They did as they were told and ran off to get the bedrock.

"I don't need any of your healing gooble goo, I'm fine," said Shaine.

The two lizards came back with the bedrock. Charmey wasn't kidding when they called it a bedrock. It was a big rock that was shaped like a hospital bed. Flax lifted Shaine up and put him down on the bedrock.

"Here you go your majesty," said Flax.

"Do not worry, Sire," Granate told him, "Charmey will have you fixed up in no time."

"I'm not badly hurt," Shaine said being stubborn. "It's just a few cuts. I'm perfectly fine." Charmey gave him a gentle frown.

"You're not hurt you say?" Charmey asked.

"Yes," answered Shaine.

"Ahh, I see," said Charmey in a smooth voice. He lifted up his cane and gently poked Shaine in the side.

"OW!" shouted Shaine.

"You see?" said Charmey, "You're hurt, and you need medical attention right away."

"But …" said Shaine. Charmey poked him again.

"Okay!" Shaine went pale. "I get it!"

"No more backtalk," said Charmey. "Now stay still while I put some goo on you." Before Shaine could say anything, Charmey began putting on the blue and slimy goo.

"Aww yuck," Shaine whined.

"Stop your complaining," said Charmey. "It just smells a little like fish."

Boy did it ever. The smell was really strong.

"There," said Charmey as he wiped his hands. The goo was glowing all over Shaine's body. It was amazing. The goo was actually making his wounds heal and disappear as we watched.

"Thank you, Mister Charmey," Shaine said sincerely.

"No problem, my boy," said Charmey. He walked over to me and held my hands. "I'm sure your wife here, Miss Sylvia, was worried about you. You sure are a pretty thing, aren't cha?" His smile widened. "No wonder the Dark Prince wanted to marry you."

"Oh no, I'm not his wife," I told him.

"No, we're not married," Shaine said at the same time.

"Really?" Charmey looked from me to Shaine, back and forth. After staring at us for a few seconds, he let go of my hand and started to wander off. "Hmm … that's too bad. You two make a cute couple."

Shocked, Shaine and I looked at each other, blushing. Then we quickly looked away from each other. It made me feel glad that Charmey thought Shaine and I made a cute couple. We do seem to have a lot in common. And he does have everything that a girl could ask for. What was I saying? He was just a friend. Wasn't he? I wondered what Shaine thought about Charmey's comment? Charmey stopped walking and turned back around to us.

"Will you be staying for the Dancing Feast?" asked Charmey.

"The Dancing Feast!" shouted Flax.

"I love the Dancing Feast!" shouted Granate. "Food and dancing all night."

"And girls," added Flax.

"Wow, that does sound like a lot of fun," I said. "You know, besides the girls part."

"We can't stay for the Dancing Feast," said Shaine as he got up. "We still have to get to the carriage and get some sleep if we want to find Princess Sylvia." He started walking away. "Now let's go."

I looked over to Flax and Granate. I could see in their faces that they wanted to stay, but they did as they were told. As they walked slowly behind, I passed them and walked with Shaine.

"How far is the carriage from here?" I asked. He thought about it for a moment.

"I don't think it's that far from here, actually," replied Shaine.

"If the carriage is not that far away, then why not stay and rest here for the night?" I asked. "I mean we can have some food to eat and have a little fun before we head out tomorrow." Shaine stopped walking. He looked at me. Then at Flax and Granate who looked very hopeful. He closed his eyes and sighed.

"Fine, we'll stay for the night." He nodded.

"Yay, we're staying for the feast, we're staying for the feast." Flax and Granate jumped up and down.

"Excellent," said Charmey. Two lizard men came up to Shaine and me and gave us each a basket. "Now you two can go pick some fruit while the rest of us get meat and decorate the place." Everyone scattered to their jobs, including Flax and Granate. Charmey lifted his cane and pointed. "Fruit's that way." With that said, he walked off.

"Well, we better get moving," I said as I walked in the direction Charmey had pointed out for us. "Come on Sparkles."

Sparkles trotted after me. I turned back to find Shaine still standing there in a daze.

"You coming, Shaine?" I shouted. His attention came back to me.

"Yeah, I'm coming," he said as he caught up to me.

They had some of the same fruit that we had, up top, like cherries, oranges, bananas, and grapes. However, there were some fruits that I had never seen before. One fruit reminded me of blueberry. It tasted like a blueberry, but its colour was aqua blue. Another fruit was round and the size of a lemon. It was a yellow-orange colour with black spots. Was it even safe to eat? Guess I'd have to see what Charmey said. As I carefully picked a spiky, green fruit, Sparkles started jumping up and down around me, almost making me drop my basket.

He whined. Poor thing must have been hungry. None of us had had any food for almost the whole day.

"I'm sorry boy," I said to him, "but I don't have any cookies with me."

Sparkles whined again as he put his head down.

"I've got some food for you, boy." Shaine bent down and opened his hand, revealing cookies. Sparkles raced over to him and started eating the cookies.

"Where did you get those cookies?" I asked as I walked over to them.

"I found a few cookie trees near a little spring over there." Shaine nodded.

"Are they good?" I asked.

"Yup," Shaine answered, "They're the best. Soft, chewy, chocolate chips that melt in your mouth." He got up and pulled a cookie out of his pocket. "Here, try one."

I took the cookie and ate it. He was right. It was soft and chewy with chocolate chips that really did melt in your mouth.

"Mmm, this is delicious." I peeked over his shoulders and saw his basket. "Shaine, your basket is empty." He looked over to the basket. Then back to me.

"You guys have fun at the party." He started walking away. "Now if you'll excuse me, I have a princess to find."

"What?" I followed him, shocked. "You're going to go find her at this time of day? Are you nuts? You have the perfect chance of getting yourself killed after dark."

"I know this place by heart." Shaine spoke with confidence, but he wouldn't look at me. "You and the others don't have to worry about me."

"But you're the only one who knows how to get out of the Forbidden Jungle," I reminded him. "And if something horrible happened to you, Flax, Granate, and I wouldn't be the only ones worried about you. What about your parents? Your brothers?"

"You honestly think they care about me?" Shaine swung around suddenly to face me. I blinked, surprised at his words.

"Of course they do, Shaine," I told him. "They love you, no matter what."

"Or they just pretend to love me because they're afraid of me," snapped Shaine.

"What, because you're the Dark Prince?" I shook my head. "That's ridiculous. Just because you're called the Dark Prince doesn't mean they believe those rumors. They know who you are. They're your family."

"Oh yeah!" Shaine stopped walking and spun around to face me. "If my family really knows who I am, then why did my brothers have to keep their fiancés away from me because my parents thought that I would try to kill them?!" I took a step back looking down. Then I looked back at him.

"You ... know about that?" I stammered. He moved away from me.

"Of course I do." Shaine looked away, his expression grim. "I knew before the rumors even started, and it's all thanks to that ... "

He stopped talking. He was really upset about this. About what his parents, brothers, and others were thinking about him as the Dark Prince. It was as if he didn't want to be the Dark Prince, but he played along with it anyway. And what did he mean by "*and thanks to that ....*" Thanks to what? Or who? I slowly walked over to him and put my hand on his shoulder. He tensed for a second, then slowly relaxed.

"Shaine," I said softly, "how did you become the Dark Prince?" He turned around to me, shocked that I asked that question. He sighed.

"It's a long story."

Sparkles yelped as he ran towards us with a basket upside down over him. He bumped into my full basket and plopped to the ground. I took the basket off him and showed the empty basket to Shaine.

"We could go put some fruit in this basket while you tell me the story."

He smiled. We each took a side of the basket and started picking fruit.

— Chapter Twenty-Nine —

The Story of the Dark Prince

Once the basket was half filled with different kinds of fruit, we squatted to pick the aqua coloured "blueberries" and Shaine began to speak.

"It all started when I was ten," said Shaine. "It was time for me and my brothers to pick princesses to marry. Sora picked Sal, Soda picked Sylvia ... "

"Wait, Sylvia was supposed to marry Soda originally?" I was shocked.

"Yeah, and they got along great until the next day." Shaine gave me a crooked smile. "She didn't want to be with him. She wanted to marry me instead, which was fine by Soda."

Wow, Sylvia had picked him, not the other way around.

"So Soda picked Flora and I was going to marry Sylvia. We hit it off great at first. We did things that other couples did. We took walks, hugged and kissed, and planned our future together. Before any of us got married though, our parents wanted us to have a little training on how to become great Kings and Queens." He sighed. "Three years later, Sylvia fell for one of my guards."

"Over you?" I was shocked.

Shaine looked away, blushing. "I got mad at her. I lost my temper and told her off. Next day she was mad at me and wouldn't talk to me. I tried everything to get her to forgive me. I gave her jewels, clothes, flowers. I even wrote a poem for her to say how sorry I was and that I would do anything for her. But nothing was working."

"I'm sorry, but I don't understand how apologizing to a bratty princess made you the Dark Prince," I said.

"I'm getting there." Shaine sighed. "But I'm warning you, once you hear the rest of the story, you'll never see me the same way again."

"I'm not that kind of girl," I said, hoping it would cheer him up. He looked at me, surprised again.

"Anyway," Shaine looked away from me. "Three weeks after the fight, Sylvia came up to me and said that she had forgiven me. I don't know what changed her mind, but I was glad that she was talking to me again. Things weren't the same after that, though. We didn't do the things we used to do before the fight, like taking walks together, and she stopped paying attention to me when I was talking to her, as if something else was always on her mind. One night, six weeks before the wedding, my father wanted to go over a few more rules before I became King of Owashia. When we were done, I headed straight to my room to get a good night sleep."

He was shivering. His hands in an angry grip. I held on to his hands for support. Letting him know that he didn't have to continue the story if he didn't want to. Shaine smiled. Then he looked away from me again.

"And then I saw her," Shaine continued. "I saw her with another man—that guard—out in the garden. Kissing." I covered my mouth with my hand.

"Oh Shaine," I said.

I guess I shouldn't be surprised that Princess Sylvia would do something like this, considering her personality. If she wanted to flirt with this handsome guard, then she was going to flirt with him, never mind that she was already engaged to be married. But still, to hear it coming from Shaine …. How could she do that to him? After all he'd done for her and given to her.

What was wrong with these women? Did they have no respect for themselves or anyone else?

"It hurt me so much to see her with another guy," said Shaine. "It made me realize she didn't really care about me, she just liked the attention and the nice clothes and jewelry that she got from being a princess." He squeezed his eyes shut, trying not to cry. "My heart meant nothing to her. It was another pretty piece of jewelry that she liked for a while until it lost it shine and then she threw it away. I couldn't stand watching another man kissing the girl that was supposed to be my bride. Something inside me went crazy right then. I wanted revenge. I tackled him and we started fighting. I managed to punch him a few times in the head and stomach, but he was older than me so he had a better chance of beating me up. I was getting really mad. I wasn't acting myself. All I had in my head was hatred and how I wanted them both gone, especially him."

His body was starting to heat up a little.

"Sylvia was screaming, telling me to stop, but I kept hitting him. I couldn't stop. I ... I really hurt him." His lower lip trembled for a moment. "Sylvia was screaming that she hated me. When our parents came in, they were freaked out. Royals can never lose their tempers, they have to think logically to govern, and I knew they saw this as a huge failure on my part. Nobody was supposed to know but ..."

"But Sylvia started a rumour of how you were forcing her to marry you when she was married to someone else and so you killed her boyfriend to fix the problem." I let my breath out in a rush.

"Precisely." Shaine stopped talking. I could feel from his skin that his body temperature was almost feverish. He was ready to talk again.

"Hold on Shaine," I said interrupting him. "You need to cool down before you continue. You're getting hotter than an oven." I got up and picked the biggest leaf I could find and folded it into a bowl. "Sparkles!"

He came running to me.

"Can you go find some water and carry it back in this bowl?" I asked.

Sparkled woofed. I gave him the bowl and he ran off to find some water.

"I don't quite understand why I'm burning up like this," said Shaine.

"It's because you're letting it all out," I said. "You've kept that day locked up inside you for so long that it's been stressing you out without you even realizing it. And now that you're letting it all out, you're being relieved of the stress."

"Well that's good," said Shaine. "I guess." Sparkles came back with water.

"Thanks, boy," I said as I took the water. I picked another leaf and dipped it into the bowl. "Here, put this on your forehead." I handed the dripping leaf to him. "It should cool you down and bring your body temperature back to normal." He did as I said and put the leaf on his forehead.

"Ahh, that's feels much better." Shaine sighed with relief after a few minutes. "Where was I?"

"You were at the part were Princess Sylvia was spreading nasty rumours about you," I reminded him.

"Right," said Shaine. "I didn't understand why people were acting strange around me until Sora told me about the rumours. It was horrible. Everyone looked at me as if I was stealing their souls. As if she hadn't betrayed me enough, our parents kept asking about the wedding. It was really irritating, but I couldn't be mad at them when they had no idea that Sylvia was flirting with other guys behind my back and that she was the main cause of the rumours. They just wanted us to be back together and happy again, like before. But I didn't want to marry her anymore, not after what she did to me and my reputation. I told my parents that I wouldn't marry a witch in disguise. Probably not the best choice of words to use at the time, but I didn't want to be with someone that would never love me."

"Didn't your parents or anybody suspect a thing about Sylvia flirting with other guys after the incident?" I asked.

"No, Sylvia is good at covering her tracks," Shaine replied. "After a few days the wedding was called off and more vicious rumours started being spread about me. I tried my best not to say or do anything to make me look like a real bad guy, but Sylvia found her ways to keep those rumors alive. Two years later, I heard that Sora and Soda were planning their weddings. I went to congratulate them, but …" He choked on the words and fell silent.

"You found out they were discussing the rumours that you meant to kill their fiancés, and how to keep Sal and Flora away from you." I guessed, hoping I was wrong.

"Exactly," said Shaine. "That day hurt me more than Sylvia cheating on me. I thought for sure my family knew the real me and wouldn't believe the rumours. My parents were so scared of me trying to kill my brothers' fiancés that they sent the girls back in their castles and my brothers had to wait to see their wives until I was gone from the castle."

"So what happened after that?" I asked.

"I gave up." Shaine looked down at the ground. "I pretended to be the killer that the people thought I was and from that day on I became known as the Dark Prince. That way I could leave the castle and be quite safe. I spent a lot of time in the Forbidden Jungle and all over—so that Sora and Soda could see their fiancés"

"So that's it." I was getting mad now. "That's how you became the Dark Prince. You let people treat you badly and get away with it and you let Princess Sylvia win."

"I tried to fight off her rumours, okay?" Shaine looked up finally and glared. "But I kept on being the Dark Prince." He looked down again. "It's my fate to be the Dark Prince."

"It's your *choice* to give up, not your fate," I told him. He thought about it for a moment.

"Do you think it's too late for me to change my reputation?" Shaine asked.

"It's never too late to change anything." We looked into each other eyes and smiled. Sparkles jumped in between us and licked our faces.

"Aww, gross." Shaine wiped his face while I laughed. I got off the log and picked up one of the fruit baskets.

"Come on, Shaine," I said as I started back to the tribe. "Let's get this fruit to the feast."

"Right." Shaine took the other basket and followed me.

— Chapter Thirty —

The Dancing Feast

Wow, Flax and Granate's tribe sure liked to grub down. The table that we ate on seemed to stretch forever and it had every different kind of food that you could ever imagine. Chicken, roast beef, lamb, and a rare meat they called chika. There was fish, fruit, vegetables, and a ton of sweets. I ate chicken, fresh fish, cherries, rice, and peas while the boys stuck with their meat. At least Shaine had some salad. Sparkles chowed down on his cookies and milk. Flax, Granate, Shaine, and I all shared the aqua berries together. The aqua berries were delicious. They were sweet and juicy—so juicy that they stained our tongues turquoise. Shaine and I kept sticking our blue tongues out at each other laughing. Once the feast was done, everyone waited for the sun to set so they could start dancing.

"Oooo, I wish the sun would hurry up and go down," said Granate. "I really want to get to the dancing."

"Oy, will you relax, Granate?" Flax rolled his eyes. "If you keep wishing for the sun to come down then the dance will be done before you know it. Besides, we still have to find some ladies to dance with."

"Oy, good point," said Granate. They both looked at me.

"Hey Layla, can we borrow Sparkles for the rest of the day?" asked Flax.

"Go ahead," I said.

"Thanks Layla," said Granate. "Come on Sparkles, let's get to work."

Sparkles ran off with them, wagging his tail. Shaine and I chuckled.

"Man, this sure has been a crazy day," I said.

"And the night is still young," said Shaine. We watched Flax and Granate try to impress a few lizard women with Sparkles for a while. "Hey, Layla."

"Yes Shaine?" I smiled and turned to him.

"I've been thinking," Shaine began. "I've been talking about myself so much that I don't really know much about you." I looked at him in surprise.

"Well, I've already told you about most of my life," I said. "What else do you want to know?"

"Well ... since you don't live with your parents, who do you live with?" Shaine asked.

"I live with my Aunt Becky and my little niece, Nikki," I told him. "Aunt Becky has been a great mother to me. She likes to cook, sew, clean, and make sure that everyone is okay. As for Nikki, she's your typical smart, girly six-year-old who wants to be a princess when she grows up."

"Of course," said Shaine. "Did you ever want to be a princess?"

"Mmm, sometimes," I admitted. "But I'm more of a worker bee than a playful kitten. Even though I had my family and friends for support, I always took care of myself. Whenever I needed or wanted something, I would work hard around the city to earn the money for it. I guess I'm just one of those independent people who like to figure out things on their own. Of course, that doesn't mean I wouldn't like a helping hand when it is necessary."

"Uh huh," said Shaine. "Tell me about your friends? What are they like?"

"Well, you've met Knuckles and Amy," I said. "Let's see ... there's Eli, who likes to have fun and always looks at the positive side of things even when they're really bad. Sheena, who dreams big and loves to party. Then there's my awesome and loyal best friend Princess Rose."

"Princess Rose, huh?" Shaine shook his head. "The princess Nilerm tried to tempt me with." He chuckled. "Actually, I'm not surprised that your best friend would be a princess. Do you have many royalty friends?"

"Well, I wouldn't say many," I said, "but I do have more royalty friends than most common people would, I guess. There's Rose, your brothers Sora and Soda, and then there's ... you." He smiled.

"Four royal friends huh?" said Shaine. "Well, that's still pretty impressive for a commoner like you to have that many royal friends."

"Yeah, I guess it is," I said. "I sometimes wonder how I managed to get a variety of friends like them."

"It's not a big surprise to me," said Shaine. "You're a rare kind of friend that's not easy to find nowadays. Honest, kind-hearted, strong, and loyal. You know when to talk and you walk the walk. You're a trustworthy friend that doesn't want our money or fame. The only thing you want in return is friendship. We can be ourselves around you no matter what we're like. You not only allow us to be ourselves, but you encourage it. That's why you have more royal friends than any other commoners could have." I smiled, looking down.

"Thanks Shaine," I said. We looked into each other eyes and grinned at each other. The huge fire was just being lit.

"Ooo, the bonfire is up," said one of the lizard people.

"Come on, let's go get a spot," said another lizard.

I stood up and ran to get a spot on the dance floor, too. Then, I realized Shaine wasn't with me. I looked back to see Shaine still sitting on the bedrock, arms crossed. I ran back over to him.

"Hey Shaine, aren't you coming to dance?" I asked.

"No, I don't dance." Shaine shrugged.

"You can't or you won't?" I raised my eyebrows. Before he could answer, Charmey's voice interrupted him.

"Alright, everyone." He clapped his hands. "Get into your positions and start dancing." The music was playing and everybody was dancing.

"Well, I'll be right over here if you change your mind," I said as I pointed. "Come on Sparks!"

Sparkles barked as he followed me.

We got into our positions and danced. The song we were listening to was called "It Takes Two to Dance." The lyrics weren't that bad, and the beat was good, too. I did spins and twists with Sparkles at the beginning. Once he ran off to go dance with Flax and Granate though, I really started to move—from jazz hands and high kicks, to hip-hop flips, and slides. Shaine looked very impressed by my dancing. He said he didn't want to dance, but I bet he was a pretty good dancer too. I danced right in front of him and sang my own verse to the song.

> *You can be at home*
> *All by yourself*
> *But there's a world outside*
> *For you and me.*
> *You can try to discover*
> *The whole wide world*
> *All on your own.*
> *Just remember though*
> *That it takes two to dance.*

"It takes two to dance," everybody sang.

"It takes two to dance," I sang.

"It takes two to dance!" everyone sang again.

"It takes two to dance!" I sang as loud as I could.

"Woo, sing it, sister!" shouted Mister Charmey. Shaine raised his eyebrow. Then, he got up and smiled.

"Keep up with me, if you can," said Shaine as he walked by me. I smiled and followed him to the dance floor.

"Haha!" Mister Charmey laughed. "Now this is a party.

I was right. Shaine was a really good dancer. We did twists and turns, slides and leaps. He was so good at dancing that I almost had to catch up with him at times. Almost. Soon, instead of doing their own dancing, everyone followed along with us and we all sang to the song. Then the music slowed down. Shaine put his hand out. I grabbed his hand and we slow danced together.

"Wow, these past few weeks have been crazy," I said.

"Isn't it always crazy up there?" asked Shaine.

"Maybe in other towns and cities," I said with a shrug, "but not in Jurassic, which is pretty weird considering it's a big, populated town."

"Well, what about adventures?" Shaine raised an eyebrow. "You must have some interesting stories?" I giggled.

"Well, I do have some good adventures up there," I admitted, "but nothing compared to what has happened down here. Don't get me wrong, I love Jurassic, but ... it's always the same. Kids playing at the playground, parents watching their kids to make sure they don't get in trouble, the gossip, girls going shopping, boys trying to hook up with those girls, and ...."

"And partying?" Shaine smiled.

"Right," I said. "Every once in a while, a bank robber or jewel thief shows up, but if you want adventure, you have to find it."

"And you didn't find it?" Shaine sounded a bit disappointed.

"No," I said. "This time, the adventure came to me." He smiled. I smiled back. "Actually, I think I'm going to like it here if I can't get back. It's beautiful, most of the people are friendly, and there's always something new to do here."

"You're not going back?" Shaine sounded so shocked and happy. I looked at him weirdly. Had he forgotten what he'd told me?

"Well, there's only one way for me to get back home, but it's impossible to reach you told me, and that my best option would be to stay down here with you guys," I said. "Isn't that what you said?" He blinked as if he were in pain for a moment.

"Right," said Shaine.

"Alright everyone," said Charmey, "Let's party loud and proud."

The music got loud with everybody screaming. I covered my ears along with Shaine. He said something to me, but the music was so loud that I couldn't understand a word he was saying.

"What!" I shouted.

"Do you like cheese?"

"Why do you want to know if I like cheese?" I shouted. He rolled his eyes.

"Just follow me." He grabbed my hand.

The further we went into the Forbidden Jungle, the less I could hear of the roaring music.

"Shaine, where are we going?" I asked.

"Simple," said Shaine, "I'm taking you to my secret place."

— Chapter Thirty-One —

Glowing Lake

"Are we almost there?" I asked, trusting him to guide me to his secret place.

"Yes, we're almost there." He tugged me along. "Now, no peeking."

"I'm not peeking," I told him. "My eyes are closed, I promise."

"Watch out for the log," Shaine warned me quickly. But I had already tripped over it.

Shaine caught me again. I squeezed my eyes tighter as my head was now lying on his chest again. He helped me get back on my feet. "You okay?"

"Yeah, I'm fine," I said. "Thanks."

"Here, let's walk together." Shaine pulled me against his body and held both of my hands this time. We walked slowly towards his secret place. "You know, for someone who's not a D.I.D., you sure are clumsy."

"Hey, everyone has their days," I said. "It's a good thing you're always near to catch me though."

"Yeah, who knows where you would have been today if I wasn't around." I could hear the grin in his voice.

"Hah, cute." I wanted to tell him that he was wrong, but the truth was that he was right. I had my moments when I tripped over something, but I was not a clumsy person. What was it about this day that was so different from the rest? I felt so different when I was with him. Like I could be myself. I mean

I'm always myself with my friends and family, but with Shaine though, I was still the same person and yet I showed him a side of me that I had never showed to anyone. A side of me that I didn't even know. But what made Shaine different from everyone else? Why was my feeling for him greater than for any other friends I'd made? What was this feeling that I had?

"We're here," said Shaine. He let go of my hands and held my arms. "No peeking."

"I've got it, I've got it." I laughed. "No peeking."

He let go of me. I could hear him slowly moving forward. If this feeling I had for him was true, did he feel the same way about me?

"Okay," said Shaine, "you can open your eyes now."

I did as he said and opened them. It was beautiful. Past the trees and bushes was a glowing lake. It was incredible. The lake wasn't too big, but it also wasn't too small. It was perfect and glowing a soft blue.

"Wow," I said as I walked over to the lake. "This is amazing."

"I'd thought you'd like this spot," said Shaine as he came up behind me. He pointed over to the right. "And over there in those hills, there is a small cave where I go to relax and get away from all the chaos. And to make my brothers feel safe." He sounded sad.

"Getting away from all the chaos huh," I said. "Guess that means you come here all the time?"

"Yeah, you could say this place is like my second home," said Shaine. I put my fingers in the glowing lake and quickly took them out.

"Oh," I said surprised, "It's warm." I took a closer look at the shinning water. "How come the lake is glowing?" He took a step closer to the lake and pointed to something in the water.

"You see that light blue thing over there?"

"Yes." I squinted at it. It looked something like a small boulder.

"It's called a glowstone," said Shaine. "They're just ordinary rocks by day, but by night they glow as brightly as they can to scare away water bugs and other creatures." I raised my eyebrow.

"Why would a rock need to scare anything away?"

"Because unlike any other kind of rock, these glowstone rocks are edible."

"Edible!" I said.

"Yeah," said Shaine, "Each one its own dessert taste. Gummy bears, brownies, ice cream sundaes—that's what they taste like."

"Okay," I said. "Then what's so scary about their glow?"

"It's not how scary the glow is, it's what it can do to you," said Shaine. "Although it is radiante, the light of the glowstone is also a poison shield to protect itself." I gasped.

"Is it even safe to be around it?" I backed away.

"Don't worry, it's not a toxin you breathe," said Shaine. "If you eat the glowstone while it's still glowing, then you'll be dead." I sighed with relief.

"Good to know." I put my hand in the water. The simultaneous warmth and coolness of the water felt good.

"You want to go for a swim?" Shaine asked. "This is probably the best time to do it." I looked at the lake. Then at him.

"Sure, why not?" I grinned.

"Cool." Shaine walked over to the other side. "Hey, Layla, do you remember our conversation? You know, the night we were on the balcony?"

"You mean where you caught me singing?" I dipped my feet in the water. "Of course, how could I forget?"

"Well," said Shaine as he eased half his body into the water with his clothes on, "I think I finally figured out what type of girl I'm looking for."

"Oh," I said, feeling excited, yet cool at the same time. This is it. I was going to find out if he felt the same way about me that I did about him.

"Yeah," said Shaine, "but I think you should tell me what type of guy you're looking for first."

"What?" I swallowed. "Why do I have to go first?"

"Because it was your idea," Shaine explained. "And since I am a gentleman, I only have two words to say, 'ladies first.'" I rolled my eyes.

"Fine, I'll go first," I said. I went into the water with my clothes on, too. "The type of guy I'm looking for must be smart, strong, and brave."

"That's all?" Shaine sounded a bit disappointed.

"No, it's only a part of what I want in a guy," I told him. "But I'm not telling you any more until you tell me something." He smiled.

"Alright then," said Shaine. "What I'm looking for in a girl is brains, kindness, and not a total D.I.D." I giggled at our joke and swam a step closer to him.

"Sweet, kind, not afraid to be himself, and will love me for me," I said. He swam a step closer to me.

"Brave, stands up for herself, not afraid to be different, and is beautiful both inside and out," said Shaine. This time, we both swam to each other.

"Works hard, has a sense of humour, but is serious when he needs to be," I said.

"Always supportive, likes adventure," said Shaine. We hung on to each other, floating in the water. He leaned his forehead against my forehead. "And I don't know about you, but I'm really attracted to blondes with light brown streaks." I smiled. He did feel the same way for me. I looked into his eyes.

"Well I'm really attracted to guys with crimson eyes," I said.

Without any hesitation, we closed our eyes and kissed. We had to break to catch our breaths every minute, but we kept pressing our lips together. He was really strong and passionate. He made me feel special. One of a kind. Princess Sylvia was a fool to leave him for her other boyfriends. All of the girls were fools. Everyone else might have seen him as an evil person when they looked into his eyes. But in his eyes, I saw … love.

— Chapter Thirty-Two —

ALE3000: aka Alejandro

I felt the warmth and light of the sun rising. I slowly blinked my eyes and opened them. I was lying on a rock with stacks of hay under me and a blanket over me. I leaned over to find Shaine on the ground, curled up and also covered in a blanket, but it was too small for him. You could see his face and legs. Why did he take the little blanket instead of the big one? He must have given me the bigger one so that between us I wouldn't be so cold. How sweet. I watched him sleep. He was so relaxed. At peace with the world. It was adorable.

"Will you please stop staring at me?" Shaine asked. I rocked back on my knees and elbows, not expecting him to be awake. I glared at him.

"What's the big deal?" I asked. He opened one of his eyes.

"Because it's hard to sleep when there's a beautiful girl watching me."

I smiled. My cheeks were going red. I slid off the rock and cuddled against him. I wasn't exactly sure what Shaine and I were now. Still two acquaintances, best friends, or a couple? We hadn't talked about it much after our kiss. We'd just gone to sleep.

"Where did you get the blankets?" I asked.

"I made a little torch and went looking for the carriage," Shaine explained. "I eventually found it and brought some blankets back here."

"Why didn't you just go back to camp and get some blankets?" I asked.

"Nah, it was getting crazy over there," Shaine answered. "Besides, I like going for a stroll, even if it's in the dark.

I giggled.

"Hey Shaine?"

"Yeah?" He smiled at me.

"About last night," I said.

"Mmhmm."

"Where does our kiss leave us now?" I asked curiously. He sat up, making me sit up along with him.

"Ahh, well," Shaine began.

I heard Sparkles' echoing barks.

"Sparkles!" I shouted.

Sparkles' barking got louder. Then he raced up, jumped on me, and licked my face. I laughed.

"Nice to see you, too, buddy," said Shaine as he petted Sparkles.

"Hey you guys!" said Flax as he and Granate ran towards us.

"What are you guys doing here?" asked Granate. They were soaking wet.

"We got tired, but it was too noisy to sleep at the camp." Shaine shrugged. "So we came here."

"Oh." They both nodded.

"Why are you two soaking wet?" I asked. They looked at themselves.

"Oh, you see once we're done dancing, we have a water fight at the end," explained Flax. "Probably should have mentioned that before. Too bad you missed that. "

"Yup, you two missed a good party." Granate started dancing around. Shaine and I got up. He gave Flax and Granate the blankets and pointed in the direction where we needed to go.

"Right, if we're done here," said Shaine. "We have a princess and an Overlander to find."

"Yes Sire," said Flax and Granate. With that said, they ran off in the direction Shaine pointed.

Sparkles followed them, barking. We sighed with relief.

"You want to talk about this later?" I asked. He looked after the departing Flax and Granate. Then he looked back at me.

"Yeah, maybe it would be better," said Shaine. "In the meantime, though ... " He put out his hand. "There is something important I would like to ask you." Smiling, I took his hand and we began to walk.

"Yes Shaine, what is it?"

"Well I'm not sure how to put this into words." He hesitated, "Actually, I never thought I would ever ask this question again, but I'm going to." I stood in front of him with my other hand on his cheek.

"Shaine, you don't have to be afraid," I told him. "Just ask me." He took my hand off his face and held it.

"Right, here goes nothing." He looked down and closed his eyes as if he needed a moment to think. He looked back at me. "Layla."

"Oy, your majesty, Layla!" shouted Flax as he, Granate, and Sparkles ran back to us. Shaine and I spun around to stand side to side, our hands locked together behind our backs as they ran to us. "What's the hold up? You two are walking so slowwwww."

I knew Shaine and I had big smiles, like little kids trying to hide the broken lamp.

"Uhh, are we interrupting something?" Granate asked.

"No." We both lied at the same time.

"We're just taking our time," I said.

"Because who doesn't love the beauty that nature gives us," said Shaine. Flax and Granate were grinning and clearly didn't believe us. Even Sparkles gave us a face that said *yeah right*. We stopped grinning.

"Right, less talk, more walk," said Shaine. "Let's keep moving, people." Still looking at us weirdly, Flax and Granate turned around and walked on to the carriage again.

"Did I miss something?" Granate whispered loudly to Flax.

"Don't worry, I'm confused too," Flax whispered loudly back.

We looked at each other and smiled. Shaine and I followed the others, still holding hands behind our backs. Two hours later, we arrived at the carriage.

"Aww, finally," said Flax, "we made it."

"Where's Alejandro?" Granate asked, scratching his head.

"Alejandro?" I asked confused.

"He's our auto-driver," Shaine explained.

"Oh," I said. Then suddenly a blue hologram appeared. He had a pointy nose and black eyes. He wore a top hat over his straight, medium length hair. As for his clothes, they definitely looked like what men like him had worn in Jurassic 800 years ago. He wore laced shoes, long slinky pants, and a long coat with puffy sleeves, three buttons, a round neck collar, and a belt over his coat.

"Well excuse me," said the blue hologram.

I jumped nearly a foot.

Sparkles yelped as he leaped into my arms.

"Well it's about time you all showed up," said the blue hologram. The hologram was talking to us. Talking right at us. Like a real person. "What took you so long anyway? One minute Prince Shaine was here taking some blankets and gone the ..." The blue hologram saw me and was stunned. "Oh ... well that explains the blankets last night."

"Oy, quit your complaining, Alejandro," said Flax.

"And the Prince goes by the name of the Dark Prince," said Granate.

"Oh my, now that's a nickname I would hate to grow up with." Alejandro smirked.

"It's alright you guys," said Shaine. "He can call me by my first name if he wants to."

"What?" Flax's jaw dropped.

"That's not fair," Granate whined. "He gets to call you by your first name but we can't."

"Who said you couldn't call me by my first name?" Shaine asked. Flax's and Granate's eyes widened.

"Uhh … I don't know," stammered Flax.

"What Flax said," Granate rolled his eyes.

"Look, I don't care if you call me the Dark Prince for the rest of my life or not," Shaine told them. "But if you want to go back to calling me Prince Shaine, I'm okay with that too." Smiling, Flax and Granate bowed down to him.

"Yes Prince Shaine," they both said.

"Ohh, how adorable," Alejandro said sarcastically. "If we're done figuring out what to call whom, I suggest we get going to Besha before Princess Sylvia and this Knuckles character head for their next destination."

"Right, but driving the carriage will take too long," said Shaine. "So change the carriage into a Jeep."

"Righty O, Sire," said Alejandro. He disappeared and the carriage and horses turned into a Jeep.

"Whoa." I was amazed. "I've got to get me one of those ALE3000 things." I got in the back with Granate and Sparkles while Shaine and Flax climbed in the front.

"Flax, you take the wheel," Shaine ordered as he got into the passenger's seat.

"Yes your majesty." Flax quickly walked over to the left side of the Jeep and took the wheel. He pushed a button. "Alright Alejandro, do your stuff." The engine roared and the car started shaking. Alejandro appeared on the dashboard screen.

"Welcome to the ALE3000 Jeep," greeted Alejandro. "Please keep your hands and feet inside the car, no drinking or eating in the car, and most importantly, don't tear up the tires. I just got some new ones after you and Granate ruined my last set."

"Hey, it was an accident," said Flax.

"Yeah, I didn't want to run over that cute little squirrel," said Granate.

"Right, now that we've gone over the rules," said Alejandro, "enjoy your ride to Besha."

"Take it away Flax," Shaine ordered.

"Yes Sire," said Flax.

"Wait a minute, what happened to safety first?" I spoke up quickly.

But Flax had put his foot on the gas and we drove off. I held on tightly to Sparkles, expecting to fall out of the Jeep without any seatbelts. But I didn't. Nobody did. How was that even possible?

"Not to worry, Miss Layla Jenkins," said Alejandro. "You have your seatbelt on, you just can't see it. Why? Even I'm still trying to figure out that one myself."

"Well, I like it because now I can stand up to stretch without having to worry about falling out of the car," said Granate. He stood up to show us. "See." Then some sort of force sucked Granate back into his seat. "Ouch."

"Will you please stay in your seat," said Alejandro. "What kind of example are you setting for the rest of us?"

"Grr … bad," Sparkles barked, "bad example." Flax and Shaine laughed while I looked at him, startled. Sparkles talked?

"I couldn't have said it better myself," said Alejandro. Granate mumbled something, but I couldn't hear him.

"Am I the only one that's freaked out by Sparkles talking?" I asked. Shaine turned around to look at me.

"There's nothing to be afraid of," said Shaine. "It's normal for a cookie to learn how to talk."

"It is?"

"Yes it is," said Alejandro. "It's what makes them different from dogs or any other kind of animal. That, and the fact that you'd think that because they're fat and fluffy like Shiba puppies, they'd get fatter the older they got because of all the cookies they eat. But it's quite the opposite. When your Sparkles is all grown up, he'll look like a greyhound."

Now even I found that hard to believe. With the way Sparkles ate cookies and as chubby as he was, I didn't see how it was even possible? Then again, this place didn't seem to be based on our science.

"Oy, when we get to Besha, what are we going to tell Antoine about Layla?" asked Granate.

"Right, we're supposed to kill her along with the other two," said Flax.

"Oh dear," said Alejandro.

"Leave Antoine to me," said Shaine. "He obeys my orders first, remember?"

"Okay, death is out," said Flax, "but we still get to punish Knuckles, right?" Shaine looked back up front to answer his question.

"Hmm, maybe a few lashes." Shaine smirked. "But if he wants Princess Sylvia and she wants him so badly then he can have her."

"What?" everyone else shouted.

"You're letting the princess go?" asked Granate.

"Yup," said Shaine, "that way I won't have to deal with her anymore."

"But Prince Shaine, you can't become King unless you get married," Alejandro reminded him. "And your parents have set the date for the royal wedding."

"Well then," said Shaine, "I guess I'll have to find another girl to marry." I leaned over his seat.

"I'm glad you're letting my friends off the hook," I told him. "But just to let you know, Knuckles will never learn anything from this."

"Everybody has something to learn," said Shaine, "Whether it be today, tomorrow, or even twenty years from now. Besides." He turned his head to look at me. "Who said I wanted Knuckles to learn a lesson?"

He made a good point. Princess Sylvia also needed to learn that she wasn't always going to get everything she wanted by using her looks. And Knuckles was the guy to teach her that.

"If you don't mind me asking, Sire, but what's with the change of heart?" Alejandro sounded curious.

"Not a change of heart," said Shaine, "just not letting Sylvia's rumours win." He smiled and winked at me. I smiled back and winked at him. As we stared at each other, everyone else looked at us, confused.

"What's going on?" Flax asked Granate.

"I don't know," Granate answered, "I'm so confused."

"Oh, you two bumbling idiots," said Alejandro, "I'm an A.I. hologram with no emotions and even I know what's going on." He paused. "Hmm ... well it looks like we're halfway there. Are you speeding again, Flax? Remember what happened last time you were speeding."

"No, I am not speeding like last time," Flax snapped. We all laughed at Flax's comment.

"Well since we're halfway there, you may as well speed it up," said Shaine.

"As you wish, Sire." Flax stepped on the gas.

I was finally getting closer to Amy and Knuckles. When I got my hands on those two, they were gonna wish that they had never messed with me.

"Oh dear," said Alejandro, "You better slow down Flax because there're ... other cars comin ... your ... wa ..." The screen turned into static and we lost Alejandro.

"Alejandro!" Shaine shouted, "Alejandro!"

Then the screen went black. And on it glowed the same green symbol that had been on the weretar's forehead.

— Chapter Thirty-Three —

Fighting off Clint Once and for All

"Hello Shaine, Layla ... others," said Clint. I could hear the boys growl under their breath. "Did you miss me?"

"What do you want, Clint?" Shaine roared.

"Calm yourself, Dark Prince," said Clint. "I'm only here to talk to you and the girl."

"For the last time Clint, I am not going to marry you," I told him. "Now go bug someone else. Take a hike."

"Oooo, somebody's got a temper." Clint snickered. "Me likie." Ewwww.

"But hey, I'm not the only one who wants to talk to you two. How rude of me." Three other Jeeps appeared on the road behind us. One on each side and one behind us. We were trapped.

"Hello Shaine and Layla," said a familiar voice as we looked to the left. "Long time no see."

"Nilerm!" I shouted.

"I thought I'd drop by," said Nilerm. Chains with grappling hooks fired from the three Jeeps and locked into ours. Our Jeep skidded around.

Flax yelled as he struggled to keep control of the car. He took his foot off the gas. Now Clint and his crew could drag us wherever they wanted to.

"You two better hope that I don't get my hands on you," shouted Shaine, "cause you're both dead meat."

"Ah-ha-ha, I'd watch your tongue, Dark Prince." Nilerm

leaned out the window of his Jeep. One of Clint's men threw an axe at Shaine, but it hit the car door instead. "You don't have the authority to threaten me now."

"Nilerm, what have you done to Jurassic?" I clenched my fists.

"Oh, nothing much," said Nilerm. "I'm just taking over the kingdom and will scatter the people everywhere."

That monster.

"I have to admit though, I was worried about you. I've attacked Jurassic for two weeks now and there was no sign of you trying to stop me. I thought you were dead. Guess you've met the Dark Prince so you were too busy trying to save yourself and your friends."

"You won't get away with this, I swear it," I said.

"Promises, promises," said Nilerm. "Speaking of which, where are the other two Overlanders?"

"Exactly where you want them to be," said Shaine, "in Besha with Princess Sylvia."

"Really?" said Nilerm. "Well that's no fun. I thought Knuckles would last a little longer than that." I growled. "Oh well, I'm still glad that you two are alive. Especially you, Layla." He pulled a gun out of his blue jacket and pointed it at me, laughing his crazy laugh. "Because now I finally get to kill you myself!" Clint grabbed the gun away from him.

"Hold on," Clint said confused. "What do you mean now you get to finally kill her yourself?"

"What do I mean?" Nilerm tried to grab his gun back. "You stupid outcast, it means I'm going to kill her! What else could I mean?"

He tried to grab the gun away from Clint again, but Clint had a good hold on it and pulled Nilerm closer to his face.

"But that's my wife to be," said Clint. "You can't kill her."

"Look pal, we had a deal," said Nilerm. "If I took you to where the Dark Prince was, I could kill anyone I wanted along the way." Struggling, he managed to twist the gun out of Clint's hand. "Now back off. I haven't been waiting for this moment to kill her since the day she came to the castle just so you could ruin it!" Nilerm took a shot, but I was already diving for the floor of the Jeep, we all were, and he missed me. Clint punched him in the face and he dropped the gun. Two of Clint's men grabbed Nilerm by the arms.

"Boys!" Clint shouted to his crew behind our Jeep. "You know what to do!" They picked up Nilerm.

"Wha ... what are you doing to me?" Nilerm struggled fiercely. "Let go of me this instant."

The two men threw him into the Jeep behind us. The chains from that Jeep released our car and the rearmost Jeep stopped moving. What was going on? What were they going to do to him?

"Cry for help in three ... two ... one ...," Clint counted down. Then we heard a shrill shriek as Nilerm screamed. Clint smiled.

"Ahh, I love the sound of someone screaming for their life," said Clint.

"You're sick," I told him.

"Thank you," Clint said proudly.

"Can't you get out of this?" Granate asked.

"No, the chains are too deep in the car to get out," Flax explained. "Plus it doesn't help that Clint here has taken control of the car."

"Okay boys," said Clint as he took the driver's seat. "Let's ride!" They sped up. They were going so fast that we had to sit on the floor.

Sparkles barked frantically.

"Okay Layla," shouted Clint over the roar of our speed, "you have two options. One, you can marry me and live."

When was he going to get it I wasn't going to marry him? I despised him.

"Or two, you can die with these people as we run you off the cliff."

I looked ahead to see if he was telling the truth, and he was. Not far ahead, there was a cliff waiting for us. Only this time there was no secret underground world to give me a second chance to live.

"This is nuts," said Flax.

"What do we do?" wailed Granate.

"We have to get their chains out of our car." Shaine looked grim.

"And we have to get Alejandro back so we can get full control again," I added. Shaine and I looked at each other and smiled.

"You thinking what I'm thinking?" Shaine asked.

"Way ahead of you," I said.

"What's the plan?" asked Flax and Granate.

"Flax, Granate, help Layla cut off the chains while I hack into the ALE3000 and get the Alejandro software back," Shaine ordered.

"Yes Prince Shaine," said Flax and Granate nearly in unison. While Shaine hacked into the ALE3000, I grabbed a hacksaw from the Jeep's built in toolbox and Granate grabbed a pair of bolt cutters, to cut off the chains.

"Back!" shouted Clint's men as they pushed us down with their spears. Their Jeeps were so close to ours that only a couple of feet separated the vehicles. "Back, back, back!"

"How are we to work on cutting the chains if they're pointing their spears at us?" Flax asked in annoyance.

"We need a distraction," I answered.

"I've got one!" Granate turned to Sparkles. "Ready to bite some bad guys?"

"Grr … yes!" Sparkles barked.

"Good cookie," said Granate.

He picked Sparkles up and he showed them his teeth. I couldn't believe what I was seeing. How many teeth did he have? His mouth looked like a miniature white shark. When Clint's men saw Sparkles' teeth, they hesitated. He lunged at them, broke one of their spears in half, and spit it out.

"Back off, outcasts," said Granate as he made as if to throw Sparkles into their Jeep. "This cookie has teeth and he's not afraid to use them."

I couldn't believe that a mere cookie had scared them, but Flax and I worked hard to cut the chains. They didn't give us enough time, though. Once Clint's men saw us working on the chains, they got over their fear and pushed us back to the floor of the car.

"Whoa!" shouted Granate.

Sparkles yelped as he went down on the floor with us.

"That didn't last very long," Granate said, a bit disappointed.

I realized that a holster mounted at the rear of the front seat held a gun. "Hey Flax, how scared would they be of a gun?" I asked him.

"Considering they've probably never heard the sound of a gun before in their lives, they'd be freaked out," replied Flax. "The outcasts don't have guns."

"Perfect," I said. "Listen up, and listen well. When I have Clint's gang distracted by the gunfire, you two each take a side of the car and cut off the chains. Once the chains are cut, I'll blow out their tires. Got it?"

"Yes, ma'am!" Flax and Granate gave me sort of a salute.

Wow, I never thought they would agree to do my orders. Now that I could get used to. I'd gotten hold of a nice, familiar style of handgun. Getting up, I shot into the sky a couple of times to scare them.

The outcast men wailed as they ducked down to the floor.

"Where's that coming from?" In his own car, Clint ducked down to the floor.

Flax and Granate worked hard to cut off the chains. The Jeeps were swerving around. I started aiming at the tires. Bull's-eye. The tires blew up and both the Jeeps spun out.

"Noooooo!" Clint screamed. They were spinning towards us.

"I'm in," said Shaine as he got back into Alejandro's system.

"Hit the brakes, Flax."

Flax turned around, hit the brake, and swerved to the right as hard as he could. Clint's car glanced off the side of our Jeep as they rolled past us, still spinning in circles. The third Jeep was still behind us, chasing us. And the cliff was just meters ahead!

"Stop!" I shouted.

"I think I'm going to be sick," said Granate.

The wheels locked up and the Jeep skidded sideways as Flax stood on the brakes. "I can't stop in time," he yelled. "We're gonna fall off the cliff!" Shaine looked down, obviously thinking quickly. Then he pulled a weird gizmo from his pocket.

"Hold on to this." He gave Flax the weird gizmo as we skidded across the last few feet of dusty ground. At the edge of the cliff, the car teetered for a moment and slid over.

I screamed as I clutched Sparkles.

"Layla, grab my hand," said Shaine as he put his hand out.

I grabbed his hand and we were falling. This was it. We were doomed. All I could do now was wait until I hit the ground. Suddenly, we all jerked to a stop. The Jeep continued to fall out from under us, until it hit the ground and exploded. Looking up, I saw Flax and Granate dangling just above me. A thin cable stretched from Flax to the top of the cliff.

"That was a close one," said Flax.

"Oy, you can say that again," said Granate.

Shaine hung on to Granate and I hung on to him

We were alive. That weird gizmo that Shaine gave to Flax was a claw hanger, he later told me. A claw hanger is like a rope that you used to climb mountains. You could extend the claw hanger as far as you wanted, plant it, and then reel yourself up to the top. Seconds after our car blew up; the other two Jeeps tumbled over the cliff, spiraling down to the ground to explode as well. The third one must have stopped in time and retreated.

"Reel us up, Flax," Shaine ordered.

"Yes Prince Shaine," said Flax.

While reeling us back up, I asked, "Do you think they're ... dead?"

"I don't know," Shaine answered. "But if there are bodies down there, then they're dead." When we got to the top, he helped me up. We let go of each other's hands and smiled at each other. It was over. We didn't have to deal with Clint, Nilerm, or any other thugs anymore. Jurassic was safe from Nilerm. "Let's keep moving, before something else happens."

"Yeah, like another weretar," said Flax.

"Or we run into another bunch of outcasts," Granate added. Walking ahead of Shaine, we all kept moving.

A voice roared. I turned around to see Clint leap onto Shaine from behind a scraggly bush.

They both rolled over the edge of the cliff, fighting madly.

"Shaine!" I screamed.

I ran back and bent down over the cliff. Looking downwards, I could only see a glimpse of him trying to get out of Clint's grip. I went on the edge of the cliff and started to climb down.

"Layla, where are you going?" Granate tried to grab me.

"To help Shaine." I shoved him away.

"No, it's too dangerous, Layla." Flax was grabbing at me, too.

"I don't care." I pulled free.

Sparkles barked and started to follow me.

"No, stay here, boy," I told him, "I'll be right back." Then some of Clint's men appeared out of nowhere and grabbed him.

Sparkles whined; trying to struggle as one of Clint's men gripped him.

"Sparks!" I shouted. It looked as if Clint and a few of his men had bailed out of their Jeeps in time. Granate grabbed the man holding on to Sparkles from behind. Sparkles jumped out of the man's arms and Granate threw him. Flax and Granate were wrestling Clint's gang.

"Go, Layla," said Granate. Flax threw the claw hanger to me.

"We've got your back," said Flax. When I started to climb

down, two of Clint's men dropped a noose over my shoulders and pulled me up.

"Whoa!" I said as I was dragged back to the top. I stood my ground, but the two men tried to pull me towards them. I was getting irritated. Shaine was down there. I didn't know if he was dead or alive, and Clint was down there with him. Shaine could be in trouble, and I was stuck with these two here.

"Let me go!" I put all my weight into a huge tug on the rope. They didn't expect me to fight back, and all three of us fell over the cliff.

As I fell, I quickly pointed the claw hanger toward the top and took a shot at the cliff wall. The claw caught into the cliff. I hit the rock face and the other two, still holding onto the rope around me, hit the rock too. They let go of the rope around my shoulders and fell.

I looked around for Shaine. But no luck.

"Dude, you really need to get a new hobby," said a familiar voice.

Shaine. I looked harder for him until I found them both. They were on a natural shelf that jutted from the side of the cliff and they were fighting. I noticed something on the cliff just beyond Shaine and Clint. It looked like a staircase up to the top. I was too far above them though. So I let go of the claw hanger and continued to climb down.

I had a better look at them now. Clint was sweating and had a few bruises, but Shaine looked worse. How could Clint be winning? I mean Clint was older and bigger muscled, but I knew Shaine could take him. Clint went for a punch. Shaine dodged it and circled around him. Clint turned, angry and frustrated.

"Stop running and fight me!" Clint screamed.

Shaine wasn't fighting? Why wasn't he fighting?

Clint went for another punch, but Shaine dodged it and ducked away again. Clint fell on his knees, tired and worn out. In my head I was telling Shaine to fight back, this was the perfect time to knock him out and get away from him. But Shaine just stood there, watching Clint pant.

"Darn it, why won't you fight me?" Clint asked. "You think you're better than me, huh? Is that it?"

"No, that is not the reason why I won't fight you," Shaine answered. "I won't fight you because you're fighting for the wrong reasons."

"Fighting for the wrong reasons?" Clint stared at him. "That's ridiculous."

"That's what makes us different." Shaine faced him, breathing hard himself. "You think fighting is the only way to get what you want: whether it be getting food, more land, girlfriends, or showing who's top dog. I fight when I need to, which is to defend myself, my people, and the ones I love."

"Oh really," said Clint with a sneer, "that's a lot of sweet talk coming from the Dark Prince." Shaine growled.

"I am not the Dark Prince!" he shouted, "and there are other ways to get the things you want in life, Clint. But this ... this is not the way you're going to win peoples' hearts."

I was getting close to them. Clint smiled. He got up and walked slowly towards Shaine.

"I'm very disappointed in you, Shaine." Clint shook his head. "But hey, it's your funural."

"You mean funeral," Shaine corrected him.

"Stop confusing me with your words," said Clint. "Since you won't fight for yourself, it'll be easy to kill you."

"Then I'll fight for him," I shouted as I jumped towards Clint. I kicked him in the face and he crashed to the ground.

"Ahh, my nose!" He put his hand over his bleeding nose.

"What did you do to him?" Shaine asked.

"It's just a bloody nose," I told him as I grabbed him by his hand. "Now come on, let's get out of here before Clint here gets back up."

We climbed to the first part of the stairs and we ran up.

"Thanks for the save back there." Shaine smiled at me. "I thought I was gonna be a goner."

"Well you wouldn't have almost been a goner if you'd fought him back," I said a bit irritated. "Why didn't you fight back?"

"Because, like I told Clint, he was fighting for the wrongs reasons," explained Shaine.

"Oh," I said like I hadn't said that before, "and what was so wrong about this that you couldn't fight back?"

Shaine stopped running, making me stop too. I turned my head and looked at him.

"It was to see who got the girl," said Shaine. "You." I blushed a little at what he said. Then I smiled.

"Good answer," I said. Suddenly, a green blob flashed above us.

Shaine pinned me back against the wall with him.

Bits of rocks came crumbling down on us. Shaine quickly pulled me behind him just in time to avoid a boulder that almost hit us. He was looking down. I did the same. Clint sprang out of nowhere and was on the cliff stairs right behind us. His hands glowed green and his eyes burned red.

"Shaine, what's wrong with him?" I asked a bit scared now.

"Let's just say he's finally released the monster in him," said Shaine.

"Alright Shaine, you have two options!" Clint roared with rage. "You either fight for the girl." His hands were glowing even more. "Or you back off!"

"Alright, alright, I'll fight you," said Shaine, "but at least give the girl a chance to get out of here first." Clint thought about his suggestion for a minute.

"Fine," he finally grunted.

"What?" I glared at him. "No way. I'm not leaving you with this psycho here." Shaine turned around and put his hands on my shoulders.

"Don't worry, Layla," Shaine told me softly. "I'll be fine.

Besides, if we both can't go find Knuckles and Sylvia, at least one of us should go looking for them."

I wanted to disagree with him, but nothing came out. Instead, it was the opposite. "Alright, you win," was all I could say.

He helped me climb up to the next step of stairs and I ran upwards. By the time I was almost at the top, I looked down to see if Shaine was still alive. And he was. But he wouldn't last long with Clint trying to clobber him. Clint had sure changed into a monster completely. His hands were glowing more brightly, his entire body had turned black, and it created a dark shine around him. Every time he tried to hit or kick Shaine, I heard a crack of thunder. I could feel the vibration in the whole cliff when Clint hit something. I couldn't let him kill Shaine. He might have felt that he was unwanted, but his people, his family, friends, and especially I needed him. I looked back up.

"Flax, Granate!" I screamed. But there was no answer. "Flax, Granate!"

I heard Sparkles' wild barking.

"Oy, is that you Layla?" shouted Granate.

"Yes, it's me," I answered. "Are you two alright?"

"Yeah, we're fine," shouted Flax. "What about you and Prince Shaine?"

"I'm alright," I shouted, "but Shaine won't be if Clint keeps pounding him at this rate. Can you guys throw down a weapon for me?"

"Sorry Layla, but Clint's outcast men took off with all their weapons and we don't have any," Flax shouted.

"All of them!" Oh no!

"Yeah," shouted Granate. He appeared at the top of the stairs with a small tree in his hand. "The only thing we have left is this small little tree."

"Oh Granate, why did you pull out that tree?" Flax shouted.

"I like it," Granate replied. "It's the cutest little tree I've ever seen. I think I'll plant it in the garden at the castle."

"Yeah, but now we have to plant another tree to replace it!" Flax shouted.

"Whoops." Granate hung his head.

I looked back down where Shaine was. He was on the ground, bruised and bleeding. Clint was stalking towards him, lifting a massive fist for a final strike. Thinking quickly, I looked back up to Flax and Granate.

"That'll do," I shouted. "Toss it down."

"But I like this tree," he shouted. "Are you sure you don't want just a plain old rock?"

"Granate!" I screamed.

"Oh, will you just give her the dang tree," Flax shouted.

"Fine." Granate looked at the tree with sadness, then he threw it down to me. "Here ya go, Layla."

Catching the little tree, I ran down the nearly vertical stairs as fast as I could without falling to my death. I just hoped I could get down to them in time, before it was too late.

"Any last words?" Clint stood over Shaine.

"I do," I said. I jumped down to them and went over to stand in front of Shaine. "Why don't you pick on someone your own size?" I held the little tree in front of Clint. He smiled with confidence.

"You think you can stop me with that?" Clint laughed.

Shaine must have figured out what I was planning because he got back on his feet. "What makes you think she's using that little tree to fight you?"

Clint was confused with his comment for a moment. Then he smirked, probably thinking that Shaine had finally lost it.

"This is just too easy." Clint snickered.

As I pretended that I was actually going to attack him with the little tree, he did exactly what I was hoping he would do. He swung at me with his glowing green fist, but I quickly twirled back toward Shaine just in time for Clint to miss me. His fist hit the ground and the stairs split in two. Shaine quickly swooped me into his arms, jumping up the stairs to get to the top before the rock crumbled under us. Behind us, with a roar, the whole stairway gave way and slid into the abyss.

"Noooooo!" Clint bellowed as he fell.

We were almost at the top, but the crumbling of the rocks caught up to us too quickly. He made one swift jump and tried to reach the ledge of the cliff, but we weren't close enough. I closed my eyes and tucked my head under his head, waiting for gravity to pull us down. But it didn't happen. We weren't doing anything. We were just holding still. Did I die so quickly that I didn't even notice?

"Hey guys," said a familiar voice, "what's up?" I opened my eyes and looked up, and smiled.

"Eli," I said with joy.

— Chapter Thirty-Four —

Second Chance

"Layla," Eli sounded surprised but happy to see me as he helped us up. "Man, am I glad that we found you."

"We," I said, a bit confused. Back up on the top, I saw Sheena.

"Sheena," I said as I ran over to her.

"Layla," said Sheena as we hugged each other, "I'm glad you're all right."

"Same here," I said. We let go of each other. "I wasn't sure if I was ever going to see you two again. How did you two get down here?"

"It's not that pretty," Eli warned me. "Plus it's not just me and Sheena. Half the people of Jurassic are down here too."

"What?" My mouth dropped open. "Oh my gosh, what's happened to Jurassic?" He sighed.

"After you disappeared along with Amy and Knuckles, I went to town to stop Nilerm from destroying it," Eli began. "When I got back to town, hundreds of buildings were destroyed and the castle was on fire."

"But Princess Rose got out of the castle just in time," said Sheena, "along with Matt and their parents."

"Thank goodness," I said. "Speaking of disappearing, did you happen to run into Amy and Knuckles?"

"Well, we found Amy a few minutes ago," Sheena said.

"But Knuckles wasn't with her," said Eli. "Where is he anyway?" I looked over to Shaine.

"Hopefully, still in Besha." I sighed.

"Then we better get going before they realize we're on their trail and run off again," said Shaine.

"Wait, he's where?" asked Sheena.

"And who's your new friend?" Eli asked as he walked over to Shaine. He put out his hand. "Hi, I'm Eli. My friend here is Sheena."

"Shaine." He and Eli shook hands.

"I'm Flax."

"And I'm Granate."

"Whoa, they're lizard people living down here." Eli freaked out. "Cool."

"Uhh … nice … to meet you," said Sheena uneasily as she hesitantly put out her hand.

Granate shook Sheena's hand while Eli grabbed Flax's hand and pumped it up and down. After a couple of seconds, Flax pulled his hand away from Eli.

"Now that we've introduced ourselves," said Flax, "let's get going to Besha."

"But we don't have a car anymore," grumbled Granate. "So how are we going to get to Besha?"

"I guess we'll have to walk then," I said.

"But if we walk all the way it'll be too late to catch Knuckles and Sylvia," said Shaine.

"Or, we can use our Jeep to drive to Besha," Eli suggested. Then he frowned. "There's just one problem." He and Sheena walked to their Jeep. So we followed them. At the Jeep, he turned around to face us. "It only seats five people."

"Which means one of us has to stay behind," said Flax.

"Actually, two of us would have to stay behind if you count Sparkles," Granate suggested. "Right boy?"

"Grr … right," barked Sparkles.

"Yeah, well Sparkles doesn't count," said Flax. "So it's back to one."

Sparkles growled and bit Flax in the leg.

Flax yelled and jumped around trying to shake Sparkles off his leg.

Granate bent over with both hands on his knees, laughing.

"Eli, is that Jeep from your hometown, Jurassic?" asked Shaine.

"Actually no, Sheena and I found this Jeep sitting around in the middle of nowhere," replied Eli. "So we fixed it up and took it for a spin."

"Well this should be a bit easier then," said Shaine as he pulled something out of his pocket. Walking over to the Jeep, he took out the broken up, regular ALE and replaced it with the ALE3000. "There." Then suddenly, Alejandro appeared, not looking so good.

"Holy crap." Eli freaked and stepped behind Sheena and me. "What the heck is that?"

"Will you relax, Eli?" Sheena told him, "It's just a hologram."

"Alejandro, can you make this Jeep bigger for us?" Shaine asked.

"No problem Sire," replied Alejandro.

The Jeep expanded into a bigger car. Sheena and Eli hugged each other, a bit terrified at what they had seen.

"Yeah, a talking hologram that does crazy things to a car ..." Eli looked very nervous.

"Oh my, and I thought we were going to become such good friends," Alejandro said sarcastically. Sheena and Eli had their mouths open, speechless. Confused, Alejandro looked at Shaine. "Did I miss something?"

"No, not really," said Flax.

"Clint just hacked into your computer system and tried to use it to kill Shaine," said Granate.

"Ahh, so the usual then," said Alejandro.

"Right," said Shaine. "Let's hurry and pick up the lovebirds."

"Lovebirds?" Sheena tilted her head.

"Clint? Death?" Eli's eyebrows rose. "What have you been doing down here, Layla?"

"It's a long story," I told them. Their eyes widened, full of curiosity. "Don't worry; I'll explain everything on the way to Besha."

With that said, we all got in the new Jeep and drove off to Besha. While we were driving, I explained everything to Eli and Sheena about what I'd been doing since I ended up down here. I told them how Nilerm had made a deal with Shaine to hand our Princess over to Shaine in marriage, but then betrayed his promise and sent me, Knuckles, and Amy off a cliff, bringing us underground. About how Knuckles ran away to Besha with Shaine's fiancé, Princess Sylvia, and Amy had tagged along with them while Shaine, Flax, Granate, and I had been looking for them. I told them how we had run into Sparkles and Clint, the outcast tribal chief's son who was trying to get me to marry him and wanted to kill Shaine.

"Wow." Eli looked amazed. "You've sure had a busy week."

"I can't believe Knuckles is doing this." Sheena sounded horrified.

"Yeah, you'd think he'd learn from the last time he hooked up with a princess," agreed Eli.

"Ugh, don't remind me," I said. "We just barely got out of that one."

"He's done this before?" Shaine turned to me.

"Well," said Sheena.

"Ehh," said Eli.

"Yes," I answered.

"My, my, my, you Overlanders are the strangest and rudest people I've ever met," said Alejandro. Sparkles barked at Alejandro. Then he jumped back up on me and licked my face. I giggled.

"Heh yeah, I don't think you're one to talk about strange things," said Eli.

"Speaking of strange things, you were telling me before how you and Sheena got down here?" I asked.

"Right," Eli continued, "I notice the backhoes were herding the people over to a certain place. So I ran over to our hang out—that's where we all go when we're done our missions," he told Shaine. "I wanted to see what was going on. When I finally got up there, I saw the backhoes herding everyone into a huge cave that I swear I'd never seen in my entire life."

"There aren't any caves around Jurassic," said Sheena.

"Nilerm probably hid it from the rest of us when he stumbled upon the cave." Eli suggested.

"But Nilerm's not good at hiding things," said Sheena, "especially big things like this."

"Maybe he was better at hiding things than we thought," I suggested. "What did you do after you saw the cave Eli?"

"Well, I yelled at the backhoe drivers to stop," Eli continued to speak. "Of course they didn't. But when I tried to go save the day, someone hit me on the head from behind and everything went dark. The next thing I knew, it was daylight. Sheena was hovering over me, freaking out."

"I was so relieved when he came to!" Sheena took his hand. "Anyway, I told him that Nilerm had pushed us and half of the citizens through a huge, long tunnel that brought us back outside to a very strange place."

"And the citizens, what were they doing?" I asked.

"Same as always," said Eli. "Running around all over the place, freaking out, screaming for help. They also kept banging on this stone wall that closed the tunnel on this end, like that was any help."

"Stone wall?" Shaine's eyes narrowed. "What did it look like, the stone wall?"

"Uhh … Just the same old thing that you see in the movies," Eli replied. The boys were confused. Giving them a look for not knowing what he was talking about, Eli started over again. "You know, the big, huge stone walls that have a bunch of written words in a language that you don't understand. And I really didn't understand those words. It was like a new language that I'd never seen before."

"Eli, any word that you don't understand is like a new language to you." Sheena rolled her eyes.

"No, I'm serious, Sheena," said Eli. "These words were just a bunch of shapes: lines, dots, swirls, squares, diamonds, and this crazy circle with a star in the middle."

"The Ecoclispe Wall," said Shaine in a tone of shock.

He wasn't the only one that went into shock. Granate, Flax, and even Alejandro wore scared faces. Like something dangerous had been released.

"Oh dear," said Alejandro.

"Shaine, what's the Ecoclispe Wall?" I asked nervously.

"The Ecoclispe Wall is what keeps your world separated from our world," Shaine explained.

"So that's what the words mean," said Eli, a bit disappointed.

"That's what the Ecoclispe Wall is for, but the words are your ticket to death," said Shaine.

"Death." I was trying not to panic.

"Remember the Overlander book," Shaine reminded me.

Of course, how could I forget that writing? "*If you run into an Overlander, take them to your home and kill them immediately,*" I recited out loud. Eli and Sheena "eeped."

"Yeah, that sounds about right," Eli said uneasily.

"Relax Eli, nobody is going to kill you," I told him.

"Yeah right, how do you know they're not going to kill us?" asked Eli.

"Because, I'm still here." I gave them a weak smile.

"Hmm, good point." Eli nodded.

"Seriously, do you Overlanders have *any* manners?" Alejandro obviously felt insulted to be thought of as a killer.

"How long have you two been down here?" Shaine asked.

"Uhh … Probably the same length of time as Layla has," Sheena answered.

"Have the words turned red?" Shaine asked.

"They change colours?" Eli looked impressed. "Cool. What does red mean?"

"It means you're lucky that you're not dead yet," Shaine replied.

"Oh," said Eli. "Well, what does white mean?"

"White!" everyone except for us Overlanders shouted.

"Yeah, that's what I said," replied Eli.

"How long have they been white?" Shaine looked worried.

"Ahh, I don't know, I think maybe for a couple of days." They all looked even more worried now.

"What does it mean Shaine?" I was worried, now. He looked down and hmmed. Then he looked back at me.

"The Ecoclispe Wall has given you a second chance to get back home," said Shaine. "But once it stops shining white, you're stuck down here forever."

"Seriously?" Eli looked scared.

"How long does everybody have left to get back home?" I asked.

"From the sounds of it, only a few hours," replied Shaine.

I brought my feet up on the seat and tucked my head into my knees, forcing Sparkles to sit beside me. I had let Rose down. I had let my people down. Heck, I had let my whole country down.

"How could I have let this happen?" I tugged at my hair. "I was the next Royal Commander. I was supposed to prevent this from happening, but I didn't. I've given Nilerm what he wanted. Now Knuckles is out there with Princess Sylvia doing who knows what else and we'll only be able to get a quarter of the people back to Jurassic." I stopped talking, trying to hold the tears back.

"Hey, don't worry about it, Layla." Eli was obviously trying to calm me down. "Like Shaine said, we still have a few hours to get back home."

"Yeah, with you back in charge, we'll find Knuckles and get everybody back to Jurassic in no time," Sheena agreed.

I looked at them both. They really believed I could fix this. I put my head back on my knees.

"But what if I fail again?" I said.

"Everyone has to fail at something at some point, it's what makes us human," said Shaine. "But we can choose to learn from our mistakes and move on, or we can give up and stand still, wondering if we could have done something to fix it."

He was right. Of course, he used my advice on me by switching around the words, but he was still right. This was not the time to give up now, especially when everyone was depending on me. I looked at Shaine and smiled.

"Thanks for the advice, Shaine."

"No problem." Shaine winked at me. I looked over to Eli.

"So if you and Sheena are here, who is with the citizens?" I asked.

"Well, there's Amy and Commander Lino," Eli answered.

"That's great," I said. "Now we can call Commander Lino on

the walkie-talkie and tell him to get everyone ready to go back into Jurassic while we pick up Knuckles."

"That's a great idea," said Eli.

"Yeah, too bad we left our walkie-talkie's behind," Sheena said in annoyance.

"It's not my fault." Eli gave her a look. "I know I put a pair of walkie-talkies in the Jeep while I was fixing it."

"Well obviously you didn't." Sheena crossed her arms.

That was weird. I know sometimes Eli can be a little forgetful, but when it comes to safety matters, he would never forget to bring something that important along. "Where there's a plan A, there's always a plan B," I said. I sat up and bent over the front seats. "Alejandro, can you communicate with anyone with any kind of equipment?"

"Hmm, well I've never done it before, but it shouldn't be a problem," said Alejandro. "Like giving candy to a baby."

"Uhh, I think you mean like taking candy away from a baby, Alejandro," Granate corrected him.

"No, that can't be right because then I would sound like a very mean hologram. I mean honestly, who would take candy away from a baby?"

"I think the point of the saying is that it's easy to do," said Flax.

"Oh, so you think it's easy to take things away from a baby do you?" Alejandro huffed. "Well what if the baby alarm goes off? Then you're in big trouble with the mother now aren't ya?"

"Baby alarm?" Sheena looked confused.

"Do you mean crying?" asked Shaine.

"Yes, that's what I said, the baby alarm," said Alejandro in annoyance.

"Are you sure we can count on him to contact Commander Lino?" Eli whispered to my ear.

"Yes," I replied.

"Now, who would you like me to call?" asked Alejandro.

"To Jurassic walkie-talkie code 18KL0T12N," I said.

"Righty O, then," said Alejandro. He dialed up the code and we waited for Commander Lino to respond.

"Here, switch seats with me." Shaine helped me to switch seats so I'd be closer to the screen.

"Thanks." I smiled at him.

"Woohoo, I knew you could figure it out," said Eli.

"So once we get hold of the Commander, how do we open the door?" asked Sheena. "That thing's got to be harder to open than a jar of pickles."

"The only way you're going to get that door open is to push the Ecoclispe Wall on the other side," Shaine explained.

"Well that's going to be difficult," Sheena complained, "especially with Nilerm now in charge of Jurassic."

"No, there's got to be some way to get to the others." Eli sounded frustrated.

"Don't worry guys," I told them, "with Nilerm out of the game, everything will be back to normal in no time."

Eli and Sheena stared at me in confusion.

That's right, they hadn't seen what happened to Nilerm. Well I didn't see exactly what happened to him either, but I do know that whatever Clint ordered his men to do to Nilerm, it wasn't a pretty way to go.

"Uhh … it's a long story," I answered. "Let's just say that he was hanging around with the wrong people at the wrong time."

"Ohh." Their faces brightened with hope.

"Hello, is anyone there?" Commander Lino spoke from the car's screen.

"Yes Commander, I'm here," I said.

"Layla? Is that you?" Commander Lino's voice bellowed through the speaker.

"Ouch," said Granate as he, Flax, and Shaine covered their ears.

Sparkles whined.

"Oh dear, I better turn down his volume," said Alejandro.

"Oh Layla, it's good to hear your voice again!" Commander Lino's voice sounded strange.

"Sir, are you crying?" asked Eli.

"What?" roared Commander Lino, "Who said that? Was that you Eli?"

"No one said that sir," I broke in. "We all know how you're a tough guy who thinks crying is for the weak."

"You bet that's what I think!" snapped Commander Lino. "So you better remember that next time, Eli!"

"Yes sir," Eli whimpered.

"Is he always like this?" Shaine whispered into my ear.

"Yeah, pretty much," Sheena told him.

"So what can I help you with, Miss Layla Jenkins?" shouted Commander Lino.

"I need you to quickly get in contact with somebody up in Jurassic and tell them to push on the stone wall," I explained. "The one he herded you all through with the backhoes. It will open. Once they have the stone wall opened, get everyone back up to Jurassic before the letters on the stonewall stop glowing white."

"What happens if these so called 'letters' stop glowing?" shouted Lino.

"Then we're stuck down here for the rest of our lives waiting for the Reaper to come get us," I told him.

"That's definitely not a good thing!" shouted Commander Lino. "I'll try my best to get back my connections to our head-quarters and get everyone out of here as fast as I can! What about you and the others? Shall I send someone to come get you?"

"No need to worry about us, Commander," I said. "We'll join you as soon as we can."

"Right, see you later then!" Alejandro disconnected us from the commander.

"My, I'm sure glad I don't work for him," said Alejandro.

"Same here," agreed Flax and Granate.

"Ohh, how much farther left to Besha?" asked Sheena, worried.

"Hmm, not much actually." Shaine eyed the terrain ahead.

"Really, why's that?" Eli asked.

"Because, we're there." Shaine smiled grimly.

Sure enough, on the horizon appeared the town of Besha.

— Chapter Thirty-Five —

Besha

Besha was like an old, small country town. We passed old, sagging buildings crowded together, horses and wagons, even a haystack.

"This is Besha?" I was a bit surprised. It didn't seem like Princess Sylvia's type of place.

"Yup, this is the place," said Shaine.

"Come on guys, let's go find Knuckles," I said. We got out of the car, and Sparkles followed us.

"No boy, I need you to stay here," I told him. He stopped walking and sat down, clearly angry. He whined and I walked over to him and bent down.

"We need somebody to guard the Jeep so that they don't take it away. It's an important mission. Unless you think you can't handle it?" He shook his head and went from being an angry pup to a happy pup. He hopped back into the Jeep and watched it, with those shark's teeth just showing.

With Sparks on alert to protect the car, the rest of us went into Besha to look for Knuckles and Princess Sylvia. There was a mayor's house, a jailhouse with wanted signs all over the wall where the sheriff was asleep in his rocking chair, and a hotel with a restaurant downstairs, where can-can girls danced for the customers' entertainment.

"Wooo, yeah baby," shouted one of the men from inside.

"Now if I were knucklehead and the princess," said Flax.

"Where would I be?" said Granate.

"Well I'll tell you where I'd like to be," said Eli, "Over there, saying hi to the can-can girls." He started walking away. "See you." But Sheena grabbed his arm.

"Will you please focus here," she snapped.

"Alright, alright, I'm sorry," Eli apologized. "You know I get distracted easily."

Then suddenly, a man came flying out of a building and hit the ground. Another man came out of the building too, all tough and angry looking. He was your typical western cowboy, wearing a big cowboy hat, cowboy boots, a vest with a plaid shirt underneath the vest, and a silver bolo tie. He had long, brown hair, and a big, long moustache. He wasn't a big man, but he was built.

"Don't come back here now, ya hear me?" The cowboy rested one hand on his belt. "Only the toughest, strongest men are allowed at this club." I blinked my eyes.

"There," said Shaine and I unison. We all ran over to the club. The man who had kicked the other guy out saw us coming and stood in front of the door.

"And where do ya'll think you're going?" He planted his fists on his hips.

"Back off, Harold," snapped Shaine. "You've probably heard why I'm here, by now." I got the feeling gossip gets around down here as quickly as it does up in Jurassic.

"You know I'd like to help you out, Dark Prince," said Harold. He took out a large bag and shook it. "But your so-called 'fiancé' paid me more goodies to keep you away. Ya'll have a good day now."

"You can't do that to Prince Shaine," I said.

"Prince Shaine." Harold's lip curled. "That may mean something in Owashia, but this is Besha. I don't owe him, or you anything, little darling." I growled at him.

"Listen pal." I stepped forward. "My friend is in there with a girl that he really shouldn't be with. So you have ten seconds to step aside and let us in or else."

"Or else?" Harold was trying not to laugh. "Or else what? What's a little lady like you gonna do to me?"

Now he was asking for it. While he was laughing, everyone took a step back away from me.

"Keeyyeeaahhhh!" I kicked him in the stomach.

Harold choked as he went flying through the air.

Crashing through the swinging doors, he slammed into a wall and left a dusty imprint of himself on it. When he fell to the floor, dust rose everywhere. As soon as the others and I walked into the room, everyone's eyes went from Harold to us. Coughing from the dust, Shaine and I walked over to him. I grabbed him by his collar and pulled him up to face me.

"Now, what was it that you were going to say?"

"Welcome to the club." Harold's eyes bulged. "Enjoy our fresh barbecued steaks. It's on the house, ya'll."

"That's what I thought," I said.

"Now where are they?" Shaine stepped up next to me.

"They're on the third floor I swear," Harold squeaked. I let go of him and he scuttled back through the swinging doors.

"Right," I said, "Eli, Sheena, you two look for Knuckles and Princess Sylvia on the second floor."

"Roger," said Eli.

"You've got it," said Sheena. They went up to the second floor.

"Flax, Granate, you stay down here while Layla and I look for them on the third floor," ordered Shaine.

"Yes Sire," said Flax and Granate.

Shaine and I looked at each other and nodded. On the third floor, I felt really uncomfortable. There were couples kissing everywhere. I wrapped my arms around Shaine's arm. I didn't want some random guy to grab me and start kissing me.

"Sylvia!" yelled Shaine, "Get out here right now!" Then she came out of her room.

"Knuckles?" said Princess Sylvia. She stopped walking, covering her mouth in a state of shock. "Oh my gosh, Shaine, what are you doing here?"

"Don't even try to play innocent," Shaine told her.

"Wait a minute, where's Knuckles?" I asked.

I heard Eli yell. We ran down to the second floor and heard people falling down the first set of stairs.

"What's going on, Sheena?" I asked.

"I don't know," replied Sheena. "Somebody just ran into Eli."

"Ouch!" Eli yelled. We all ran down back to the first floor. Knuckles was on the edge of the stairs lying on top of Eli, who looked really ticked off. "A simple get out of the way, or even move it would have been nice instead of slamming into me."

"Fine, get out of the way," Knuckles shouted as he scrambled off of Eli and started to run. "How's that?" Flax and Granate grabbed him by the arms.

"Not very nice," said Granate.

"And in big trouble," Flax added. Princess Sylvia ran past us and walked up to Knuckles.

"I can't believe you were trying to run away," she snapped.

"Bring him outside," said Shaine. "Now!" Flax and Granate did as he said and dragged Knuckles outside. They threw him to the ground.

"Ouch!" said Knuckles. Shaine stood over him.

"I really ought to punish you for what you've done," Shaine snarled. He looked over to me then he looked away from me, closing his eyes, and taking a deep breath. "But Layla has shown me that not all of you Overlanders are bad people." I smiled, letting him know that I was thanking him for letting the Knuckles incident pass by and not starting a war against Jurassic. He smiled back and walked away from Knuckles. "Which is why I am once and for all officially calling off my wedding to Princess Sylvia."

"Wait a minute." Princess Sylvia looked shocked. "You're not going to marry me now?"

"Nope," answered Shaine, "You can marry whomever you want, as will I."

"Oh Knuckles, isn't this great?" Princess Sylvia said joyfully. She ran over to Knuckles and hugged him. "We can get married and live happily ever after."

"Whoa, whoa, whoa, I don't think so," said Knuckles as he gently pushed her away. "I am not getting married. This whole getting married at a young age kind of thing might be normal to you, but where I come from I've still got a life to live."

"But you said you were willing to give up your role as Royal Commander so we could be together," said Princess Sylvia.

"Give up your role as Royal Commander!" I shouted. "You didn't even get the job in the first place!"

"Yeah, but if I did get the job I would have." Knuckles actually looked embarrassed. "Ah, I can't stay with you Sylvia."

"What?" I glared at him. "No, you don't get a say in this."

"She's right, dude," agreed Eli. "You promised. You're pretty much messed up."

"I'm not messed up," said Knuckles. "I'm not getting married, simple as that."

"Are you kidding me?" I could feel my temper fraying.

"Knuckles, you pig," Sheena snapped.

"We've got a chance to maintain peace between our countries and you won't even do it," I said.

"Grr," Knuckles growled, "Can't the Dark Prince marry her?"

"Forget it," said Shaine.

"Look, I'm sorry alright." Knuckles looked almost ... embarrassed. "I can't do this. It's ... it's not the life I want."

"Nicole, don't do this," cried Princess Sylvia.

"Nicole?" All of us Overlanders screeched it in unison. Knuckles' face flushed. He looked away from us, blushing.

"Yeah, that's ... my real name," Knuckles said in embarrassment. We covered our mouths, trying not to laugh. But our giggles got to us and pretty soon we *were* laughing.

"I can't believe your real name is Nicole." Sheena giggled.

"Dude, your parents gave you a girl's name." Eli snickered.

I was laughing really hard until I saw Princess Sylvia. She looked really upset, like she had broken her promise to Knuckles about keeping his secret safe. The fact that he had even told her made me realize that he must really care for her after all.

"Haha, you guys are so funny," Knuckles said sarcastically. "Now let's go, you can laugh at me all the way home."

"Wait, can I have a word with you first, in private?" I asked.

"Do I have to?" whined Knuckles. I glared at him.

"Yes," I said as I grabbed him by the ear and we walked away from everyone. When I found the perfect spot away from the others, so they couldn't eaves drop on our conversation, I let go of his ear.

"Ouch." Knuckles rubbed it.

"Look Knuckles," I said, "don't marry Princess Sylvia because it'll bring peace for us or our people. But do it to face your fear."

"Fear?" Knuckles scowled. "I'm not afraid."

"Then why don't you want to get married?" I asked. He had to think about it for a moment.

"Because … because … because, I don't want to get married."

"It's okay Knuckles," I said softly trying to calm him down. "Everybody, especially the guys, freak out when they think they might have found … the one."

"The one," said Knuckles. "Whoa, whoa, whoa, I didn't say I was in love! What makes you think I'm in love?"

"Nicole," I said. "You told her your real name, Knuckles. Do you know how long we've been trying to get you to tell us your real name?" He shrugged.

"Kindergarten. I've been trying to get you to tell me your real name since kindergarten."

"That doesn't mean anything." Knuckles frowned. "Besides, she just managed to … persuade me." I raised an eyebrow.

"Really Knuckles?"

"Well, she did." I rolled my eyes.

"Well did she also persuade you to give up your job as Royal Commander?" His eyes shifted left to right, trying to not look me in the face.

"Maybe." I punched him in the arm. "Ouch."

"Don't lie to me; of course she didn't," I said, "because you told me and the others that you would never give up your title as Royal Commander for a girl. No matter how pretty she was or how much she tried to 'persuade' you."

"Well, maybe I was overreacting," said Knuckles. "Being Royal Commander isn't that big of a deal."

"Not that big of a deal?" I said. "Knuckles, you and I have been competing for Royal Commander since we joined the Royal Guards."

"Yeah, I guess being rivals for four years does seem a bit crazy," Knuckles admitted.

"Actually it's been five years." I corrected him. "But you were close."

"Right." Knuckles smiled. Then it was quiet.

"Well, since I'm wrong and there's no changing your mind," I said, "let's go home." As I was walking away from him, he finally spit it out.

"I'm not afraid to get married and become a husband," said Knuckles. I stopped and turned to look at him. "I'm afraid to become a father." I blinked my eyes, letting him know that he had my attention. "You know what I'm like with kids. I'm a bully. I don't like kids."

"Knuckles, you haven't even tried to like them," I said as I walked back to him. "How do you even know you won't like children?"

"You can't like something that you've never liked before," said Knuckles.

"Sometimes when you try something new you end up loving it." He scratched his head.

"I don't know," said Knuckles. "Taking on the role of a father is a pretty big risk." He looked over to Princess Sylvia and smiled. She beamed at him, her eyes full of love. "Then again, maybe being a father won't be so bad."

"And you'll never know unless you take a chance," I said. Looking down, he closed his eyes, trying to think about what he should do.

"Hmm," said Knuckles. Then he looked back at me and smiled. "I think it's time I took some responsibility, huh?"

"That would be nice," I said. Done with our conversation, we walked back to the others. They watched us coming back, like an audience waiting for the next scene in a movie to see what happens.

"Sylvia," said Knuckles, "I'm sorry this took so long to ask but …." He got down on his knees, putting one hand in the air and other on his chest. "Will you marry me?"

"Oh Knuckles," said Princess Sylvia as she began to cry, "of course I will." Then they did the typical hug each other, kiss and make up, and everything was back to normal.

"Okay, okay, now that everyone is happy," said Eli, "can we get going? We're starting to run out of time."

"I guess you're right," I said, feeling … strange. I turned to Shaine. "Hey, you didn't get a chance to ask me about something earlier in the Forbidden Jungle."

"Oh, right, my question that I wanted to ask you." Scratching his head, he looked away from me. He was silent for a moment, his face all full of guilt. Then he was back to normal and smiled at me, eyes hard to read. "Actually never mind, it wasn't really that important. I just wanted to ask you if you enjoyed the … Dancing Feast."

"The Dancing Feast," I said. "Yes, I did enjoy it quite much." Then we heard the Jeep's horn beep. It was Eli and Sheena.

"Come on Layla," said Eli, "we've gotta go."

"Oh." I was filled with sudden sadness. "I guess it's time to go home."

"It's probably for the best." Shaine sounded sad, too. I sighed.

"Come on Sparkles," I said.

Sparkles barked.

"Ahh Layla, you can't bring that purple thing with you." Sheena sounded disgusted.

"Why not?"

"Because he doesn't belong in Jurassic," Sheena said. "He needs to stay in his own environment." I looked at Sparkles. It was probably better for him to stay down here where cookies and milk grew on trees.

"What am I going to do, bud?" I said, "I can't just leave you." Sparkles whined.

"Don't worry, I can take care of him for you," said Shaine.

"Really?" I turned to face him.

Sparkles barked as he jumped up to Shaine.

"Whoa!" Shaine almost fell over as he caught Sparkles.

"Thank you Shaine," I said.

"No problem," said Shaine. "Now I'll have a part of you with me." I smiled. "And since we're exchanging, here." He put down Sparks and looked back at me. "Do you think you can hold on to something for me?"

"Sure, what is it?" I asked. He put his hand in his pocket and held out his fist. It was his timestone, on a golden chain.

"Oh no, Shaine, I can't take away your timestone." I shook my head.

"It's not a big deal, Layla." Shaine grabbed my hand and put the timestone in it. "Besides, I know you'll keep it safe and out of harm's way." I looked at the timestone for a few seconds, then put the chain around my neck.

"Thank you, for everything," I said.

"Just promise me you won't forget this place?" Shaine's eyes searched my face.

"I could never forget," I whispered. The Jeep beeped. Everybody was onboard, waiting for me.

"Come on Layla!" shouted Eli, "We're running out of time. We have to go." I looked at Shaine.

"I've gotta go." I petted Sparkles' head. "Bye, buddy." I heard him whine as I was walked away.

"Flax, Granate, you two take care of yourselves now."

"We will," said Flax.

"We'll miss you," said Granate as he waved goodbye.

"And as for you two, Knuckles and Sylvia." I paused by them. "Stay out of trouble."

"We will," said Knuckles.

"Goodbye," said Sylvia. As I got into the Jeep, Eli was ready to go.

"Layla wait!" shouted Shaine and ran over to us. I quickly put my hand up, telling Eli to hold on for a few minutes. He and Sheena were starting to get a bit ticked, but they waited.

"Yes, what is it Shaine?" I asked him.

"Layla, I just wanted to say ... ," Shaine said quickly. Then he stopped talking, as if he'd forgotten what he was going to say. He seemed to be thinking for a moment. What was on his mind? What does he want to tell me? He sighed. "I just wanted to say that ... I hope ... " There was another pause. "I hope you find everything that you're looking for as Royal Commander." I was a bit stunned by his words, but I knew he meant well for me.

"You too, your highness," I said.

"Goodbye," said Shaine.

Before I could say anything, Eli put his foot on the gas and we drove off. He was driving so fast that I had to close my eyes. Once he started to slow down, I opened my eyes and looked behind the Jeep. Shaine was no longer there. Nobody was.

"Goodbye," I whispered.

With that said, we went our separate ways.

— Chapter Thirty-Six —

Happily Ever After?

I was finally going home. I was going to see Aunt Becky, Nikki, and my dear friend Rose again. I was going to come back as a hero. I was finally going to take my place as Royal Commander. So then why wasn't I excited anymore?

"Layla!" shouted Sheena.

"Huh?" I said.

"I've been talking to you for twenty minutes about how thrilled you must be to start your job as Royal Commander once we get back home," said Sheena.

"Oh sorry," I apologized.

"Are you alright Layla?" Eli asked "You've been awfully quiet since we've been driving."

"I'm alright." I lied. "I've just been thinking, that's all."

"Aww, there's no need for the jitters," said Sheena. "You're gonna do great. You always do."

"Thanks, Sheena, but that's not what I was thinking about," I said.

"Really?" Sheena gave me a perplexed look. "Then what *are* you thinking about?" I had to find the right words without letting them know what I was really thinking about.

"A very complicated puzzle," I said.

"Oh, you mean the new mall arrangements?" said Sheena. "I've been thinking about that too. How are we going to be able to shop at stores with awesome clothes while looking at cute guys that are around and still be close to a food court?" Thankfully, Sheena was on the other side of me where she couldn't see my eye twitching.

"Yeah, that's it," I said trying to keep my cool.

"Well I'll tell you what I've been thinking," said Eli. "I wonder what Shaine wanted to say."

"What are you talking about Eli?" Sheena rolled her eyes. "He said he hoped Layla found everything she was looking for as Royal Commander."

"He may have said that," said Eli, "but that's not what he really wanted to say."

"What?" Sheena sounded shocked.

"Eli, are you sure?" I asked.

"Positive," Eli answered. "You could see it in his face." Sheena and I stared at him, waiting for him to speak again. "I could tell he wanted to ask you something big," he continued, "but he looked a bit terrified to ask because he wasn't sure if he was doing the right thing."

I looked at the timestone he'd given me to protect me. I knew there was something really important he wanted to ask me. But what was it?

"So I wondered what he really wanted to say."

I looked at Eli. "Well maybe if you hadn't driven off so quickly, we could have found out," I said. He looked at me, feeling guilty. Then he looked back at the road.

"I'm sorry, Layla," said Eli, "but we had to get going. We were running out of time and if we stayed any longer to wait for him to spit it out, we probably wouldn't make it back home." I put my hand on my head.

"Yeah, you're right Eli, I'm sorry," I apologized.

"Are you sure you're alright?" Sheena sounded a bit concerned now. I quickly turned to her and closed my eyes.

"Yes, I'm fine." I lied again. I opened my eyes and looked back at the timestone.

What did Shaine really want to say to me? Why couldn't he just tell me what was on his mind? Maybe he thought that even if he did tell me, it wouldn't have made a difference? Difference to what though? To stay? To leave? What? My thoughts, however, got interrupted when Sheena grabbed my arm, shaking me.

"Layla, are you listening to me?" Sheena shouted.

"Huh?"

"I said we're here."

I looked over to where she was pointing. We'd made it back to the others. I guess whatever he really wanted to ask me didn't matter now. I was going back home now to take up my duty as Royal Commander while he and the others were probably on their way back to their home by now. I was going to miss them and this place, but as Shaine said before, it was probably for the best. We lived in two different worlds and we each had our own responsibilities and duties to our countries. It was for the best ... wasn't it? It looked as if Commander Lino had gotten almost everyone back up to Jurassic. The only people that were left from what I could see were him and ... Amy.

Getting out of the Jeep, I shouted, "Amy!"

"Layla!" Amy ran over to me. She put her hands on her knees trying to catch her breath after she stopped running. "Layla, I'm so sorry for running off with Knuckles. I didn't want to, but he promised me ... "

"I'll deal with your punishment later," I told her. "Right now, we've got to get out of here."

"Well spoken, Commander!" shouted Commander Lino.

"Lino," I said, "is everyone back in Jurassic?"

"Yes ma'am, everyone!" shouted Commander Lino.

"Great," I said, "then let's get going."

"Amy, are you coming?" shouted a thirteen-year-old boy.

"Coming sweetie!" Amy shouted with joy as she ran off to him.

"Who's that?" I whispered to Sheena.

"That's Amy's boyfriend, Loomer," Sheena whispered back. "Isn't he the cutest thing you've ever seen?" Then Eli stepped between us.

"Sorry Sheena, but I think Layla here is more interested in guys that are around her age," said Eli.

"And what is that supposed to mean?" Sheena asked.

"Uhh ... so who's ready to go home?" Eli said instead.

"I am," I said helping him out.

"Great, let's go," said Eli as he pushed Sheena and I to move. Soon, Commander Lino and I watched Sheena chase Eli to the Ecoclispe Wall. Then he looked back at me.

"Hey, where's Knuckles?" shouted Commander Lino.

"Oh, he's not coming with us," I replied. "He has a commitment to make between our two worlds, which is why nobody is after us in case you were wondering."

"Well done sold ... uhh I mean Commander," said Commander Lino. "Proven yourself worthy to be a Royal Commander."

"Thanks Lino." He nodded his head and smiled.

"Come on, slow pokes, are you coming or what?" Eli shouted.

"You better watch your tongue solider!" snapped Commander Lino. "Or else you'll be the one running for twenty-four hours! And you don't want that now, do you?"

"No sir," Eli said nervously.

"Good!" shouted Commander Lino. "Now let's go home." Walking with Eli to the Ecoclispe Wall, I punched him lightly in the arm.

"Ouch." Eli smiled at me.

"That's for calling me slow poke." I teased him.

"Fair enough," said Eli. "I guess I deserved it." I giggled at him. "So how did you convince Knuckles to stay behind and get him to marry Princess ... Sylvia was it?"

"Yes, Princess Sylvia," I said. "Well, it didn't take that much to convince him actually. I just told him to face his fear and take a chance with her."

"Fear?" asked Eli a bit confused.

"It wasn't that he was afraid to get married or of becoming a husband," I explained. "It was becoming a father that scared him. So I told him that if he loved Sylvia and didn't take this chance with her, then he would always wonder if he had done the right thing."

"Ahh, so you gave him the 'what if' strategy," said Eli. I stopped walking.

"I didn't say that stuff just so I could fix up his mess," I said. Pulling out the timestone, I held it in my hands. "Sometimes when you're looking for your true love, you've got to take chances."

"Good point," said Eli as he walked over to me. He took the timestone out of my hands and looked at it. "In that case, that's some good advice." Then he looked at me. "Maybe you should take your own advice sometimes."

He let go of the timestone and continued walking to the Ecoclispe Wall. Take my own advice. What was that supposed to mean? I didn't need to take any chances. Did I?

"Come on, Layla!" shouted Sheena. "We're almost home." I took a deep breath and sighed.

"Home sweet home, here I come," I said as I walked up to the Ecoclispe Wall. Somehow, I couldn't feel a lot of enthusiasm.

Before I went inside the cave, I took one good last look at the underground world that I would never see again. The last time I would see my new friends I'd made on our adventures. I was never going to see Flax, Granate, Sparkles, and Shaine … ever again. Inside the cave, it was very dark and bumpy, but I could still see to the other side and Jurassic.

"Oh, I know you're going to love it, Loomer," Amy was saying with confidence. "The shopping, the romance."

"And let's not forget about the parties," added Eli. "Especially the one for Miss Layla, here for her first victory as Royal Commander tonight."

Everyone cheered.

I giggled at them for their excitement to go home and party. I thought I would be excited and ready to party too. But the fact is I wasn't. Then halfway through the cave, I stopped walking. I tried to keep moving forward, but I couldn't. It was as if my feet were glued to the ground. In my head I was saying *go*, but my body was saying *stay*. Like I was making a big mistake. But what? Why couldn't I keep moving? Then something came to me. I put my hand over my heart and closed my eyes. And I knew.

"Layla!" shouted Commander Lino, "Are you coming or what?" I opened my eyes and smiled. I couldn't go with them. Jurassic was not my home anymore.

"Eli, Sheena!" I shouted. "Can you two do me a favour?" They looked at each other confused. But then they looked back at me.

"Sure Layla," said Eli, "What is it?"

"As the new Royal Commanders of Jurassic, tell my Aunt Becky, Nikki, and Rose that I love you all and I'll miss you terribly," I said.

"What?" shouted Eli and Sheena in shock.

"What?" yelled Commander Lino, in shock, too.

"Layla, where are you going?" cried Amy.

Suddenly, the whole cave was shaking. Bits of rock came falling down. I looked behind me. The Ecoclispe Wall was closing.

"Oh no," I could barely whisper.

I made a run for it. I had to get through the stone wall. I had to get back to him. More rocks kept hitting me, bouncing from my arms and shoulders, but I didn't care. I had to keep moving. The Ecoclispe Wall had almost closed. Close enough, I leaped into the air, hoping that it was enough to get me out of the cave.

Eli's voice, screaming my name, was the last thing I heard as the wall thundered closed.

I coughed from the sandy dust in the air. Had I made it? Was

I still in Jurassic? When some of the dust started to settle, I saw the Ecoclispe Wall behind me. I made it! I made it back underground. And I was dirty, with a few tears in my nylons. When the dust cleared completely I realized that someone else was here. On the ground with his hands over his head. Why he almost looked like …

"Shaine?" I shouted. He looked up.

"Layla!" yelled Shaine.

"Shaine!" I ran to him.

He got to his feet and ran to me too. I leaped into his arms and he twirled me around. Then he put me on the ground, his hands on my waist while my arms were around his shoulders.

"Layla, what are you doing here?" Shaine asked.

"I couldn't go back to Jurassic, Shaine," I told him. "There are many opportunities for me to become a Royal Commander, but there's only one of you. I can live my whole life without being Royal Commander, but I can't live my life without you because I love you, Shaine. I love you." He sighed with relief and smiled.

"I'm glad to hear that," said Shaine, "because I came here to stop you. I didn't want to ask you if you enjoyed the Dancing Feast, I wanted to ask you if you would stay down here with me, but after seeing you with your friends from above, I didn't want to take you away from your old life. I don't think I can live my life without you, either, because I love you too, Layla. I love you, too." I smiled, trying to hold in the tears. He leaned his head against mine.

"So now what?" I asked curiously.

"Well, I am going to be the next King of Owashia," said Shaine, "and I do need a Queen to rule by my side. So, what do you say, princess?" He got on his knees and held on to my hands. "Will you do me the honour of becoming my wife?" I grinned, letting the tears fall.

"Yes, of course I will," I answered. He picked me up in his arms and twirled me around again.

"Did you hear that, world? She said yes!" Shaine yelled it as loudly as he could.

We were both laughing as he twirled me around again. This time when he put me down though, we looked into each other's eyes and pulled each other in to kiss. It was wonderful. It was magical.

It was the perfect ending and the beginning of my happily ever after.

THE END

Author Biography

Jenny Story was born in Yellowknife, but lived the majority of her life in Vernon, British Columbia. She then moved to Vancouver to attend the Vancouver Film School and become a 2D and 3D Animator. In addition to her work with animation, Jenny has always been an avid reader and writer, and wrote this book when she was only in high school. Despite being diagnosed with Autism, Jenny has always remained focused on pursuing her dreams and is passionate about inspiring others to do the same.

If you want to get on the path to becoming a published author with Influence Publishing please go to www.InfluencePublishing.com

Inspiring books that influence change

More information on our other titles and how to submit your own proposal can be found at www.InfluencePublishing.com

CPSIA information can be obtained at www.ICGtesting.com
Printed in the USA
LVOW04s0509020415

432874LV00004B/4/P